The Tenant

By

Victoria T

Copyright © 2024 Victoria T

ISBN: 978-1-917293-04-4

Marriage is a rollercoaster of emotions, with its highs and lows. In the beginning, as newlyweds, there's a sense of being wrapped up in each other and nothing else seems to matter. However, as life continues, it's easy to forget why we chose to be together. Sometimes, it just takes a little spark to reignite the love and make everything perfect again. But what if that spark has faded and the relationship is in turmoil? It can feel like your whole world is falling apart. The honeymoon phase doesn't last forever, sacrifices need to be made for a marriage to last, but what if the person you love the most asks you to lie to protect themselves? Would you still be willing to risk everything, even after they've hurt and betrayed you?

Rebecca Jones, known as Becks, was a thirty-seven-year-old head teacher at a local primary school. She exuded perfection with her straight, shoulder-length blonde hair always neatly tied back. Her baby-blue eyes sparkled as she spoke and smiled, showcasing her poise, elegance, and passion. Becks had impeccable emotional intelligence, keeping her thoughts and level-headedness refined. She possessed a flawless figure, being athletic, academic, and musically inclined. She was a true all-rounder who had a deep passion for creating a better world and a brighter future for the next generation. Despite her parents' disapproval of her desire to gain an education and explore the world, Becks remained determined to conquer. She was the eldest among her siblings, with two younger brothers who had no interest in furthering their education. As a child, Becks was her father's pride and joy until she married, what he referred to, as a 'pen pusher'.

Her husband, Connor Joseph Jones, was a thirty-eight-year-old accountant who was highly articulate and intellectual. He came from a privileged background, receiving a private education from the age of four. He held a master's degree in finance and business and went on to specialise in corporate accountancy. On the surface, he appeared to be the perfect husband and father, always well-groomed and sophisticated. However, there were moments when his demeanour could be snobbish – he often looked down on individuals who did not possess a higher education qualification. Connor was on the verge of taking over the firm where he'd worked since graduating from university, and life seemed idyllic for the happy couple.

Connor and Becks crossed paths during their university years, with Connor in his final year and Becks just starting her second year. Their meeting at a party sparked an immediate connection, as if they were meant to be together. Their shared interests in tennis, badminton, art, and wine brought them closer, pushing each other to excel academically and in their hobbies. Their relationship quickly evolved into something serious, leading to him proposing after graduation. They meticulously planned their future together, from securing employment to having children, with each step carefully mapped out.

Their two sons, Rory and Logan, were well-behaved and intelligent. Rory, a seven-year-old football enthusiast, resembled his father, and Logan, a mischievous five-year-old, won their hearts with his quick wit. Both boys attended the primary school where Becks taught, allowing her to balance her career and motherhood. The boys' behaviour was exemplary, displaying their intelligence through their well-groomed appearance, impeccable manners, and eloquent speech. Connor and Becks encouraged their outgoing nature, wanting them to excel and believing that the world was at their feet. They longed for a conventional upbringing for their kids and were not fond of contemporary parenting methods. They reminisced about their disciplined upbringing in the 1990s, where parents held authority and children showed respect. Both agreed that raising children in today's modern society posed challenges, and their utmost desire was for their sons to grow up as well-rounded and sensible individuals. With a structured life plan in situ, they believed they were living in marital bliss, with everything running smoothly and their home life perfectly organised. Their shared desire for a regimented schedule and minimal deviation kept them on track towards their goals, creating a harmonious family life.

In March, Connor's business partner retired, leaving him in full control of the firm, just as the new financial year began. He had a remarkable talent for numbers, effortlessly calculating everything in his head like a human calculator. His obsession with spreadsheets was unparalleled, fuelling his success in his new role. The profits started pouring in, allowing him to indulge in a new, environmentally friendly, electric car that brought him tax benefits. He also splurged on an expensive watch and multiple tailored suits, allowing him to feel on top of the world. Previously reserved and introverted, his elegance and sophistication now shone through his polished appearance. Donning stylish polo shirts and chinos on weekends, he sported perfectly groomed, gel-styled hair, and a neatly shaven face. His dark-rimmed glasses emphasised his piercing blue eyes. The scent of his designer fragrances added to his overall finesse as he confidently strolled with an upright posture and a sense of pride.

Becks also flourished in her work, excelling as a class teacher before, temporarily, stepping into the role of deputy head. It was during this time that she discovered a knack for management and decided to apply for the head position at her current school. With her start as head teacher scheduled for September, Becks felt an overwhelming sense of empowerment. She elevated her wardrobe to match her newfound authority, upgrading to power suits that projected confidence. Becks had a commanding presence, entering rooms with impeccable posture that exuded strength. Always wearing heels to school, she accentuated her calves and added height to her petite frame. While her outfits were modest, with skirts below the knee, and no display of cleavage, Becks never doubted her ability to succeed without using her physical appearance, and she disliked women who did so. Instead, she relied on her sharp mind and persuasive ability to navigate any situation. With minimal makeup, her skin tone was always complimented and her eyes stood out. Her perfectly straight blonde hair was washed and blow-dried into a stylish ponytail, and she turned heads wherever she went.

The summer holidays arrived, a delightful and warm six weeks away from their busy lives and hectic mornings. The family enjoyed two weeks in the beautiful south of France, immersing themselves in culture, art, delicious cuisine, and new experiences. They returned home refreshed, with a sun-kissed glow, and were ready to dive back into school and work.

On the eve of Becks' first day, she carefully laid out her new outfit, consisting of a beige skirt, white shirt, and matching jacket. This was complimented by her perfectly coordinated brown heels and handbag. Though she felt a touch of apprehension, deep down she was overwhelmingly excited about this new adventure.

"Are you nervous?" Connor asked.

"A little, but honestly, I'm more excited. This is everything I've ever dreamed of. I can't wait to transform the school and make it better," Becks proudly exclaimed, heading towards their bed wearing a long silk nightgown and applying moisturiser to her arms.

"You'll be amazing, I have no doubt," Connor reassuringly said, as he sat up in bed with laptop in hand.

"Are you ready to go back to the office?" Becks inquired.

"Yes. As much as I enjoyed the break, I'm eager to hit the ground running," replied Connor.

"Goodnight, my love," Becks said with a smile, kissing him on the cheek before turning over and closing her eyes.

"Goodnight," Connor replied lovingly, as he continued to work on his laptop.

Becks quickly adapted to her new position as head teacher, embodying a perfect balance of friendliness and firmness that made her well-loved by everyone in the school. She was proactive, accessible, and making a significant impact in the education field. The first half term flew by and, by October, Connor felt ready to transition to a larger home, marking the next step in their journey with meticulous financial planning for retirement and future endeavours.

On a chilly Friday evening in October, after a tiring week of work and school activities, they sat together at the dining room table. Papers were scattered across the surface, and a bottle of wine was open and ready to be enjoyed. With the children fast asleep, it was their time to discuss finances. Connor was engrossed in his calculations.

"So according to my calculations, we can comfortably afford this property. We have the deposit, the additional stamp duty and, looking at the current mortgage rates, it will cost this much per month which is affordable, and it will still leave us with this amount to invest in bonds and shares," he confidently said. His eyes were focused intently on the spreadsheet before him, his finger tracing the numbers, as he explained his findings while occasionally adjusting his glasses with his index finger. Becks peered lovingly over his shoulder.

"That's the dream home, love. Are you sure we can afford it?" Becks asked.

"We can, my love," he said reassuringly. Becks was enamoured by his financial prowess, finding it impressive and endearing. Excitedly, she agreed to move forward with their plans.

"We'll have to rent this house out to make our investments work," Connor continued

"I'll handle the rental, if you can arrange the buy-to-let mortgage, it will relieve that stress from you," Becks offered with a warm smile.

"Let's do this. I'll ring tomorrow morning and make an offer. Now is a good time. People are often more inclined to take a cheeky offer as they want the sale completed before Christmas," Connor said confidently.

"Do you think we could have the new house by Christmas?" Becks inquired with enthusiasm.

"I don't see why not," Connor concluded.

They then settled on the sofa, Becks' legs draped over his, envisioning their future in their new home. Sipping on her Chardonnay, she eagerly anticipated filling the house with cherished memories, and growing old together. As they eventually retired to bed, they engaged in their usual Friday night intimacy, finding solace in their routine and making the most of their weekends. They were happy and content and were completely on the same page, life together was effortless. Once they had made love, they put their pyjamas back on, kissed each other on the lips, then both turned away from each other and drifted off to sleep.

By early December, the house sale was complete and they were the proud owners of two homes. With their busy work schedules, they were thankfully able to move their belongings gradually. They dedicated their weeknights and weekends to transferring thirteen years of memories just four miles away. During this time, they painted, hung pictures, assembled furniture, and created new memories that were more relaxed and enjoyable. They laughed, played, and danced with their children to background music, even putting paint on each other's noses. The boys were particularly thrilled about the move, as the new house had a larger garden and more rooms, allowing each of them to have a spacious bedroom. The kitchen was impressive, with an open plan design and a large island featuring tall bar stools where everyone could gather while Becks cooked. She was incredibly excited to prepare and serve meals to her family, as it represented her dream of being a mother and a wife, living a simple and fulfilling life together.

As the Christmas holidays began, Becks and her family had settled into their new home. It suddenly struck Becks just how much stuff they had gathered over the years. She couldn't help but feel sentimental about parting with the baby items they no longer needed. On the weekends leading up to the holidays, Becks had returned to their old house to make it presentable for renting. She diligently cleaned and touched up the paintwork, and now it was time to find a tenant.

Becks contacted the local estate agent and promoted the house on social media. Despite the slow response leading up to Christmas and the lack of urgency from the agents, she remained hopeful about finding the perfect family for the beloved home. On social media, Becks received a message from Kerry Reed, a woman who seemed to belong to the upper middle class, based on her profile filled with pictures of luxurious holidays, dining at fancy restaurants, and wearing expensive clothing. Noticing that Kerry had a young daughter, Becks thought she seemed pleasant.

She contacted the estate agent and requested them to make contact with Kerry. However, the agents informed Becks that they were unavailable to meet anyone until after the New Year. Despite this, they asked Becks if she would be willing to show Kerry around the property and Becks agreed, scheduling a meeting with Kerry on the Wednesday before Christmas.

Wednesday had finally arrived, prompting Becks to drop off the boys at their football club before heading to the old house. She needed to ensure that everything appeared flawlessly clean. Right on cue, the doorbell chimed, revealing a petite and graceful woman. She wore a sleek black coat paired with a cropped jumper, flaunting black leather trousers and stylish leopard-print shoes. Fragrant notes of Tom Ford perfume trailed behind her. Her slicked-back, dyed blonde hair was held by oversized designer sunglasses, and her impeccably done makeup accentuated her plump lips which gave off a vibe of familiarity with Botox and lip fillers. She carried an exquisite designer handbag to complete the ensemble, and had parked her black Mercedes outside, adding to the overall elegance.

Becks and Kerry engaged in lively conversation for more than an hour, with Becks expertly using her interviewing skills to uncover any potential issues.

"Are you married?" asked Kerry.

"Yes, to Connor, he's wonderful. We have two young boys, Rory and Logan. I'm very lucky," Becks boasted.

"What does your husband do?" Kerry inquired.

"He's an accountant; he has a firm in town. He's a mastermind with figures, it's quite impressive to watch," Becks added.

"Very impressive," Kerry replied, smiling.

"What about you, Kerry, what do you do?" Becks asked curiously.

"My husband and I own a consultancy company, but, unfortunately, we're going through a divorce and I need a clean break, hence the move," Kerry replied.

"That must be difficult. Are you continuing with the business?" Becks asked.

"Yes, for now. I'm a director and I handle the administration side. We built it from scratch so I'm not willing to just walk away," Kerry added. "Do you work?"

"Yes, I'm a head teacher, for my sins," Becks replied, with a forceful faux laugh. The sheer delight on Kerry's face was noticeable.

"You both have impressive careers," Kerry said in awe.

"Do you have children?" Becks questioned.

"Yes, Darcy, she's twelve, going on twenty-one! They certainly don't get any easier," Kerry replied sarcastically. They both casually chuckled as the small talk continued. Becks was completely at ease as the conversation flowed freely. She couldn't help but feel positive about Kerry.

"The house comes fully furnished. If you wish to remove anything, let me know and I'll see what we want to do with it," Becks explained.

"Yes, of course. It does help to have it furnished, all of my furniture is in the house and he's refusing to leave. It would be difficult to move everything, so this is just perfect," Kerry happily replied.

Becks proceeded to give Kerry a tour of the house, leading her through each room before finally taking her to explore the garden and garage.

"I apologise for the state of the patio, it desperately needs replacing. As you can see, the slabs are cracked and some are broken, it's just the wrong time of year to change it. If you do decide to take the house, we'll get it replaced for you in the spring," Becks explained.

"That's not a problem. It's a beautiful house; I can imagine it's a sun trap in the summer and you're not overlooked at all. I'd like to go ahead, Becks; it's perfect for my daughter and me. I'll put all of my cards on the table, my husband has been unfaithful and I'm desperate to get out of the house as he can be physically aggressive, too," Kerry explained, pulling up her sleeve to show bruises on her forearm. Becks was taken aback and instantly felt empathy for Kerry. The shock was evident on her face.

"I'm so sorry you're going through this, Kerry; it's truly awful. I have no problem with you renting the property, but I need the estate agent to do your credit checks and references. They'll need to take your deposit, too before I can give you the keys," Becks explained.

"I completely understand, it's just, it's 20 December, do you think everything will be back in time for Christmas? I'd love to give Darcy a Christmas to remember, without any fighting. It's been traumatic for her. I do understand though. Do you think if you ask them, they'll send everything over today? Would that be OK? I'll pay you an extra week's rent," Kerry said. With an innocent and vulnerable expression on her face, Kerry gazed deeply into Becks' eyes, causing her to falter under the intensity of the moment.

"Let me ring them right now and I'll ask them to send everything over immediately," Becks replied with glee. After a conversation with the estate agent, they agreed to send all the necessary documents directly to Kerry. Becks then shared her phone number with Kerry and requested her to call once everything was finalised.

By the 22nd, Kerry had not contacted Becks, prompting her to call the estate agent. To Becks' disappointment, the agent informed her that they had not received any documents from Kerry. Frustrated, Becks muttered to herself about the wasted time before hanging up the phone. The next morning, on 23 December, Becks was busy with paperwork when she received a call from Kerry, who was sobbing on the other end of the line.

"Hello, Becks? It's Kerry. I'm so sorry to ring you like this. He's hurt me again, I had to go to the hospital yesterday. I haven't received any paperwork from the estate agent yet, but I still want the house," Kerry said in an emotional rant. Becks acted on a whim while Connor was at a football game cheering on the local team with the boys and his friends. She asked Kerry to meet her at the house in an hour.

As Kerry pulled up, she stepped out of her car sporting sunglasses, a white hoody and a long black coat, paired with trainers. She had a cut lip and a bruise under her right eye.

"Oh my God, is this what he's done to you? Have you called the police?" Becks asked in shock.

"No!" she abruptly answered.

"But Kerry—" Becks said. However, she was interrupted.

"No, I can't call the police. He has to have a clean police check for his line of work. I'm a director of the company, if I tell the police he'll have his licence to practice revoked and everything we've worked for will be gone. I need the money from the company when I divorce him, so I can't call them. Please, you have to help me. I also have my daughter to think of. I'm scared he'll hurt her too, he has no control," Kerry wept. Becks was hesitant to involve herself in this situation, but her strong belief in the fair treatment of women and the presence of a child compelled her to take action. As a teacher, she couldn't stand by and let this injustice occur.

Becks reached out to the estate agent to inquire about the status of the paperwork, only to discover that they had mistakenly written down the wrong email address for Kerry. As a result, Kerry had yet to receive any paperwork from them. To make matters worse, the estate agent informed Becks that they couldn't proceed until after Christmas, and also explained that the credit checks and deposit couldn't be processed until after New Year. Feeling overwhelmed, Becks asked Kerry if they could meet back at the house in two hours, requesting her to bring identification and proof of address.

Becks then got back into her car and called Connor, who, although sceptical, offered his support.

"Connor, this lady, she's been abused by her husband. She's shown up today with a cut lip and a bruised eye, she has a child – I can't turn my back on her," Becks said empathetically over the phone.

"Are you sure you want to get involved in this, Becks? Just leave her, tell her no," he swiftly replied.

"You can be so cold-hearted at times. What if it was me in this situation?" Becks replied.

"Well, it wouldn't be you because I would never do that. I can't hear you properly. Do what you feel is right," Connor supportively but abruptly replied.

Feeling determined and responsible, she devised a contract and met Kerry back at the house. With papers in hand, Becks entered the house and meticulously went over each document with Kerry.

"Hi, thank you for coming back," Becks said.

"No, thank you for helping me. It means a lot, I have nowhere else to turn, we have no family close by," Kerry replied. Moved by Kerry's sense of loneliness, Becks was determined to relieve her of any distress she could.

"I know that feeling. OK, I'll let you have the keys, but you need to read and sign this contract. I'll take a copy of your identification and proof of address. Can you transfer the deposit and a month's rent upfront? I'll send all of this to the estate agent once they reopen after the New Year. I won't charge you for this week, only from 1 January, does that sound OK to you?" Becks asked.

"Yes, of course, write down your bank details and I'll transfer the money now," Kerry said. In just ten minutes, Becks had received the deposit and a month's rent in her account. They both signed the tenancy agreement after she took copies of Kerry's identification. Becks handed Kerry the keys and left with a sense of satisfaction knowing she'd made a positive impact by helping someone in need, especially during the holiday season.

Upon returning from the football game, Connor and the boys were greeted by Becks, who'd prepared a delicious roast chicken dinner. During the meal, Becks shared with Connor the news that Kerry had paid a month's rent and the deposit in advance. He commended Becks for her kindness and successful tenant placement so close to Christmas. As the sun began to set, Becks sorted through the paperwork for the rental property, creating a fresh box file to keep everything organised. With great satisfaction, she carefully placed all the important documents inside. Just as she closed the cupboard door, Connor unexpectedly entered the office, catching her off guard.

"What are you doing?" he asked.

"Goodness! You scared me. I've made a filing system for the rental house. I think it best if I keep everything organised," she replied.

"You are wonderful, well done for doing that today," Connor said, as he walked towards her and lovingly placed his arms around her waist.

"I felt very sorry for her, it's made me realise how lucky I am to have you," Becks murmured, planting a sweet kiss on his lips.

Christmas was a peaceful affair with two overly excited young boys, still enchanted by the magic of the season. Becks made sure to enhance every aspect of the festive spirit in their new home. Connor's affluent parents, Ted and Mary, visited on Boxing Day, although their departure brought a greater sense of relief. Ted, a retired accountant, took pleasure in sharing tales of financial mishaps and advising Connor on money matters, embodying an old-fashioned demeanour where he was always right, and Mary catered to his every need without complaint. Ted was your typical older gentleman, always dressed in a stiff-collared shirt with patterned jumper over the top, and suit-type trousers. He was ready for any occasion. Connor and Ted somewhat clashed, their debates could become quite heated and their difference of opinions often resulted in Mary giving Connor a stern talking to. They had Connor later in life and had been married eleven years before their bouncing baby boy entered the world. Mary was forty-one when she gave birth and often referred to Connor as her 'gift from God'. Ted and Mary were a religious pair, providing a strict Roman Catholic upbringing that Connor had distanced himself from over the years but pretended to partake in for the sake of his parents.

Mary was always in a skirt just past her knee – she didn't own a pair of trousers – good old-fashioned pantyhose, a blouse and a cardigan. She wore a cross around her neck and often tried to fill the boys' heads with extracts from the Bible. Mary was a housewife, who frowned upon Becks' desire to go out and work. She questioned Becks' every move and constantly advised her on how to raise two young men.

"You know dear, a mother should be at home with her family. This new modern world of women having it all, it's a load of codswallop really," Mary commented, as she continued to sip her glass of sweet sherry.

"I am at home Mary. I work school hours and I'm at home during the holidays. The boys are very well grounded and are doing remarkably well at school. Do remember, I'm the head teacher at their school now," Becks replied sternly, yet with a sincere smile.

"Head teacher? When did that happen?" Mary asked in despair.

"September, Mary, did Connor not tell you?" Becks inquired, as she stared at him coldly.

"No. No, he didn't. How on earth are you expected to run a home if you're a head teacher?" Mary replied.

Well, I think I'm doing an OK job, Mary. I can manage and Connor's also here, helping to raise his sons," Becks replied.

Ted then interrupted in a loud voice, "Women should be at home, making sure the house is ready for when the man comes in from a long, hard day at the office. Why are you letting her work?"

"Letting me work?" Becks said with a raised voice.

"I think what Rebecca means to say is that times have changed. Women work, it's normal, and she's good at her job so why should I stop her?" Connor supportively replied.

"Stop me?" Becks said, as she glanced back at him.

"I mean, it's up to Rebecca. She chooses to work and it works for us," Connor continued, with a sense of nervousness.

Luckily, the conversation was shut down quickly when Becks stood up and left the living room to check on the brie in the kitchen.

"I'm sorry, are you OK?" Connor said, as he followed her into the kitchen. He came towards her, wrapping his arms around her waist.

"Every God damn time. I mean, do they not realise what year we're living in?" Becks replied, as she hugged him back.

"It's one night a year. Come on, we can do this," Connor replied, kissing her on the cheek.

"Right, it's Monopoly time! Cheese and Monopoly, what a perfect Christmas combination. Rebecca, is that brie ready?" shouted a tipsy Ted from the living room. Becks and Connor exited the kitchen, chuckling and shaking their heads, with Becks holding a beautifully arranged cheeseboard and Connor's hands resting on her shoulders. After a night of intense board game competition, the final players, as always, were Connor and Ted, who were both refusing to back down in the most intense and professional showdown ever witnessed. Mary relaxed in a chair and the boys dozed on the sofa, creating a true Christmas atmosphere with family gathered together. The following morning, after breakfast, they bid farewell to Ted and Mary, with Mary's emotional goodbyes making the boys cringe, yet they still smiled and waved like the picture-perfect suburban family at the front door.

New Year's Eve was uneventful, with the Jones family asleep before midnight, they were lost in their routine. This was followed by New Year's Day and this time it was Becks' parents' turn to make their annual visit, thankfully limited to a lunch affair. Becks was the daughter of Bob and Joan, and this visit was a very different one to Connor's parents – the two sides never saw eye to eye and consistently clashed in their outlook on life. Becks grew up in a working-class family, on a functional farm which was her father's pride and joy. Unlike her two farmer brothers, she was the odd one out, the only sibling who had left home and moved over sixty miles away. While she enjoyed the outdoors and nature, the farming lifestyle wasn't for her. Despite having a beautiful childhood with the freedom to explore the fields, Becks desired more than a stagnant life. She longed for an education, which her parents disapproved of. Determined to pursue her dreams, Becks worked two part-time jobs and applied for grants to support herself through university. Her parents, who were financially struggling but owned acres of land, made it challenging for her to become a scholar. Becks was determined to be different and sought excitement and adventure, she did not want a simple life for her children. She was always determined to break away from the traditional farming life her family embraced.

Her parents would enter her home reeking of cow manure. Her father, a massive man standing over six feet tall and weighing roughly 115kg, neglected his health by eating poorly, drinking excessively, and believing his farm work made him healthy. Wearing the same soiled jeans, brown checked shirt, and socks with holes for the last decade, his appearance remained unchanged. Her mother always appeared unkempt, with unwashed hair pulled back in a scrunchy, showing no interest in her appearance wearing loose, baggy jeans and an oversized blue shirt. It was clear they'd come straight from the farm and hopped into their car. Bob and Joan sat there, criticising the exquisite meal that Becks had painstakingly prepared, wearing sour expressions on their faces. They casually dropped off bags of dirty home-grown vegetables and three dozen eggs, barely acknowledging their grandchildren, before leaving in their twenty-year-old green Land Rover.

During dinner, very few words were exchanged. Becks was accustomed to the absence of praise or positive feedback since childhood. As a child, her academic achievements went unnoticed, with her parents showing little interest in her education and prioritising her brothers' help on the farm over their schooling. Bob and Joan felt judged by Connor and disapproved of the changes they saw in their daughter.

An almost deafening silence filled the room as Becks struggled to extract any conversation from her parents, making the whole experience quite excruciating.

"So, Dad, how's the farm going?" Becks asked.

"It's OK, hard this time of year, but we tick along, year in, year out. Thankfully, your brothers are there. I'm getting old now," Bob said, with an inverted dig at Becks.

"You know, Bob, there are a lot of developers looking for land, perhaps it's time to hang up your boots," Connor suggested.

"Son, you listen to me, you've not done a full day at work in your life. You sit there after you've pratted around with numbers all day and say you've worked hard. You don't know the meaning of the word, and there's no way in my life that anyone is going to take my land and build more bloody houses that we don't need!" Bob said in utter disgust, with his mouth full of food.

"Dad, that's not fair, all jobs are equally hard work. Yes, yours is more physical but Connor works very hard, his job isn't easy," Becks said, in an attempt to support her husband.

"Right, I knew this would happen. Joan, we're leaving. I'm not going to sit here and be spoken to like that. But let me tell you one thing young lady, accountants are for lazy people. I've been on that farm every day for the last sixty-nine years, as my father and his father before that. We've worked hard, and never needed a man in a suit to do anything for us. The food that's on your table comes from people like us. Everything you eat. If we don't do our jobs, you don't get your food, now you just think about that," Bob said, as he stood his large frame above everyone at the table.

"Dad, please, I—" Becks attempted to speak, but the mere presence of her father rendered everyone silent with fear. This was the case every time he spoke.

In a loud voice, Bob continued, "Every year we drive nearly two hours to get here, to sit in a house that looks like every other house, on an estate, no fields, for what? To be belittled and ridiculed by people who don't even understand. Well, this will be the last year, mark my words. You, young lady, have forgotten your roots. You loved growing up on that farm, you were an outdoor girl, and now look at you, with your fancy food and a husband who pisses around with numbers, living on an estate where everyone knows your business." Bob stood at the head of the table looking at his daughter in disgust. Becks' face, was a picture of pure horror. She felt like a schoolgirl again.

"Dad, please, we didn't mean anything. Mum, please, sit down, you haven't finished your food. There's desert too," Becks said, as she held her mum's hand.

"Sorry, love," Joan said, as she stood up and made her way to the front door, trailing behind her husband disappointedly. Joan turned around, hugged Becks and rubbed her back, as she struggled to hold back her tears. She kissed the boys on their heads and gave a warm smile, but she had such sadness in her eyes. Becks sympathised with her mother, feeling a strong desire to assist her. She understood that, deep inside, her mother wasn't content, but this was the only life she'd ever known. Meanwhile, Joan slipped on her boots by the entrance and walked behind

Bob, who continued to ramble on as he made his way back to the car.

"Bye, Mum," Becks said, as she blew her a kiss. Connor gently placed his hands on her shoulders in an attempt to comfort his wife.

Later that night, after tucking the boys into bed, Becks was completing her kitchen chores while Connor perched on the dining table chair.

"Every God damn year, why do we do it to ourselves? Are we the ones in the wrong?" Becks asked, as she scraped the leftover food into the bin harshly.

"No. There's no right and wrong, we just live different lives. It's our choice to live like this and not everyone agrees, but that's their issue, not ours," Connor expressed. The empathy he held for his wife was palpable. Becks possessed a loving and benevolent character, striving for optimal outcomes in all circumstances.

"I understand that, but I just feel so very sad when I can't sit at the dinner table with my father without it causing such aggro," Becks replied. She was devastated by the tension that had arisen between her and her family, and her heart ached.

"It's always hard when you choose to follow a different path, especially from your parents. We're brought up in a certain way, we know nothing other than what our parents teach us. It's only when we get out of that clutch that we experience different things, we gain a different perspective. Please, don't think anything of it, we're happy," Connor said lovingly.

"Yes. Yes, we are happy, it's just disappointing," Becks replied in agreement, as she looked down at the floor below and then suddenly lifted her head high, resuming composure.

"Come here, sweetheart, don't let this upset you," Connor said as he kissed her. He smiled lovingly, took her hand and led her upstairs. Becks smiled sincerely back at her husband, they were happy, they were in love. However, Becks couldn't shake off the pessimistic thought that lingered in her mind, questioning why everyone couldn't simply get along. She constantly had the sensation of having to satisfy two different authorities, as if she possessed two heads.

Once the offices were back in operation, her first action was to contact the estate agent. She detailed the situation and they were less than thrilled that she'd entrusted the keys to Kerry, but they acknowledged their mistake and took responsibility. They promised to reach out to the tenant and swiftly resolve the outstanding matters. To ensure everything was done properly, Becks transferred the deposit and considered the issue sorted. Becks and Connor returned to their busy work schedules, feeling like everything was under control.

Connor had begun attending the nearby gym, going consistently for two months now. After work, he would head to the gym to exercise and de-stress. Juggling the responsibilities of being the firm's boss was proving to be more challenging than he'd anticipated. However, his gym sessions were helping him clear his mind and release his pent-up frustrations, preventing him from taking it out on Becks and the kids. Becks worried about him but didn't want to make a big deal out of it, she was happy to see him excelling in his fitness regime. She'd grown accustomed to multitasking, being the one to get the boys ready for school, dropping them off on her way to work, picking them up after their activities, and then starting the routine all over again at home. The home chores consisted of preparing meals, bathing the boys, helping with homework, and ensuring they went to bed on time. She had her hands full. While she was glad that Connor had his way to unwind, she couldn't help but wonder where her escape was!

As January came to an end and February began, Becks eagerly checked her bank account, only to find that Kerry hadn't paid the rent. By 5 February, stress started creeping in, prompting Becks to reach out to Kerry with a message.

'Hi Kerry, Becks here. I hope you're doing well, I wanted to text, but didn't want to pester you. Anyway, I do hope things have calmed down for you and your daughter. I'm sorry to ask but the rent hasn't gone into the account as of yet, could you kindly look into this please?' With trembling fingers, she hesitated before hitting the send button. Then a thought crossed her mind, *Why should I be nervous? After all, she owes me money!* As she finally pressed send, she closed her eyes and gazed up at the sky, silently pleading for a swift response. Miraculously, within a mere five minutes, Kerry's reply appeared in her inbox, bringing her much-needed relief.

'Hi hun, oh my goodness, it's so nice to hear from you, the house is just perfect and we're loving living here. So sorry about the rent, I'll get it sorted now. XX,' replied Kerry. Becks breathed a sigh of relief as the money appeared in her account within an hour, instantly calming her nerves. The last thing she needed was for things to go awry and add more stress to her already full plate.

A fortnight later, on an ordinary Monday evening in mid-February, Connor found himself at the gym completely immersed in his workout routine. With music blasting in his headphones, he pedalled away on the exercise bike, sweat pouring down his face. After finishing his session, he glanced up at the ceiling, took a sip of water, and caught sight of a stunning woman. She had blonde hair in a high ponytail, captivating blue eyes, and full lips – she'd certainly caught his attention. Clad in a Lycra crop top, her toned physique was accentuated, with her sculpted abs and prominent chest. Paired with sleek black leggings, trainer socks, and matching black trainers, her fitness level was evident from her appearance.

"Hi, have you finished on here?" she asked flirtatiously.

"Yes. Yes, here, I'll just wipe it down for you," he stuttered, wiping the seat.

"Thank you," she replied, as she smiled and mounted the bike seductively. With her golden locks, slender figure, and undeniable allure, she was exactly the kind of woman he found irresistible.

With self-assurance and determination, he turned and strode away, yet found himself glancing back at her, their eyes locking as she smiled at him. Shaking off the distraction, he hurried to the rowing machine, cranked up a lively tune, and pulled the handles with increasing speed. After ten minutes of intense rowing, his heart was pounding, prompting him to stand up and quench his thirst with water.

"Hey, again," the same woman said.

Slightly startled, Connor replied awkwardly, "Oh, hi again, sorry, do you want this machine now?"

"Yeah, thanks. I'm Suzy by the way," she said, as she smiled and looked him square in the eyes.

"Nice to meet you, I'm Connor. Well, I better go," he replied, as he fidgeted with his wedding ring, put his head down, and wiped the sweat from his forehead. After heading to the changing room, he showered, changed into fresh jogging bottoms, and a crisp white t-shirt, then made his way to the mirrors to fix his hair and put on his glasses. As he gazed at his reflection, thoughts of the woman lingered in his mind before he shook his head. Swiftly, he exited through the automatic doors and, clutching his gym bag, he hopped into his car and drove back home.

He walked through the door of his house, where Becks was sitting at the kitchen table surrounded by paperwork.

"Hi, I'm home," Connor shouted.

"Hi, dinner is in the oven for you," Becks replied, without even looking up.

"Great, thanks," he said as he took his plate from the oven. He walked towards Becks with his plate balanced in his right hand, the tea towel wrapped around the plate, and kissed her head.

"Where are the boys?" Connor asked, as he pulled out his chair and sat down.

"They were playing an action hero game so I left them to it. I should go and put them to bed, actually," Becks said, as she glanced at her watch. She stood up from the table and left him to eat alone. At that moment, Connor's phone, which was resting on the table next to him, emitted a beep. It was a friend request from Suzy T. Curiosity piqued, he glanced at her picture and recognised her as the beauty from the gym. How did she manage to find him? Confused, he couldn't help but notice her stunning sexiness and allure. However, he swiftly regained his composure and decided to ignore the request.

Becks headed back downstairs to complete her paperwork and clean up the remaining mess in the kitchen. After that, she went back upstairs only to find Connor already tucked into bed.

"How was the gym?" Becks asked, as she undressed in the bathroom and brushed her teeth.

"It was good, it does help," Connor replied.

"That's great, maybe I should go, too. God knows I could do with the release," Becks said.

"Yes, you should, it's good for your mind. You just need to be oblivious to the people around you," he replied.

"What do you mean?" she asked, as she emerged from the bathroom.

"A lot of vain people in tight clothes, wandering around looking at themselves in the mirror," he said, as he laughed.

"Sounds right up my street. Are you sure you're not one of those?" she replied in jest.

"Yes, maybe, it's a little mad," he replied, and let out a small laugh. Just then his phone beeped again: 'private message request from Suzy T.'

'Are you ignoring me?' it read.

"Who's that at this time?" Becks asked.

"Oh, just Rich. He's asking about a drink later this week," Connor replied, so easily lying.

"Oh, right, you can go if you want to," she replied.

"Are you sure?" Connor asked.

"Yes. I have a mountain of paperwork to do, go ahead after the gym one evening. Goodnight, love," she said, as she leaned in and gently planted a kiss on his cheek.

With a flick of her hand, she switched off the bedside lamp, turned away, and peacefully drifted off to sleep. Connor smiled and started to reply to Suzy.

'No, not ignoring you, just not sure how you found me?' Connor replied.

'You're well known at the gym and it's not hard to find out anything about anyone these days, Connor Jones,' came the cheeky reply. Suzy's messages flooded in with intensity, capturing Connor's attention, even though he tried to keep his responses ambiguous. However, her words had an unexpected effect on him, arousing his desires. Meanwhile, Becks lay peacefully, completely unaware of the unfolding situation.

'So, will I see you at the gym tomorrow?' Suzy asked.

'Yeah, I'm there every night, same time, same routine,' Connor typed.

'Great! I might see you there. Goodnight, Connor Jones,' Suzy's reply read. However, this time she accompanied her reply with a picture of her lying in bed wearing a silk nightie. Connor reclined on his back, gazing at the ceiling above him. A wave of joy surged within him, filling him with anticipation. It had been ages since he last experienced such excitement.

As the sun rose, Connor opened his eyes to find an empty bed beside him. Becks had already showered and dressed, taken care of the boys' breakfast, and was bustling around the house, fully immersed in the morning routine.

"Connor, are you up? We're leaving!" she shouted abruptly. With a groggy mind, he slowly rose from the bed and slid his glasses onto his face. It took him a moment to clear the fog in his head and collect his scattered thoughts.

"Yes, yes, love, I'm up. Bye, have a good day," he shouted back. As he glanced at his phone, he discovered three new messages from Suzy. A mix of fear and curiosity washed over him. He'd never ventured into such territory before. With a surge of excitement, he rose from his bed, took a refreshing shower, got dressed, and headed off to work. His stomach fluttered with anticipation, a sensation he hadn't experienced in a long time. After his regular lunchtime conversation with Becks, he received two messages from Suzy, One read, 'See you soon, big boy.' He could feel something happening, but he didn't know what to do. He finished work, got into his car and called Becks on the way to the gym. He pressed Becks' number on his touch screen.

"Hello," Becks answered.

"Hi, I'm on my way to the gym. I won't be too late, I have some paperwork to do at home," Connor said over the phone.

"No worries, love, take your time. I've had a very long day preparing for this inspection, so I might have an early night if I can get the boys down," Becks replied. At this moment, he couldn't care less, all he could think about was the overwhelming desire to see Suzy once more.

Connor stepped into the gym, quickly changing into his workout attire before entering the bustling main area. A blast of cold air from the air conditioning caught him off guard as his gaze swept across the room, but Suzy was nowhere to be found. A mix of disappointment and relief washed over him as he began his familiar routine. The music blasted through his headphones, his concentration was lost in the rhythm, and he closed his eyes, focusing solely on the beat. With each pedal, he pushed himself to the limit, his determination evident. As he gradually slowed down, he opened his eyes,

"Boo!" said a voice.

"Jesus Christ!" Connor let out a loud yell as he came face-to-face with Suzy.

"Sorry, I didn't mean to scare you," she said, laughing.

"No, you didn't, I was just in the zone, you know. Here, let me wipe it for you," he replied in an attempt to play it cool. He took out his earphones and went to wipe the seat.

"No need, I'm happy to sit here after you," she said as she touched his upper arm and stared at him again. With a smile, he turned around as she mounted the bike. Post work out, he did the usual shower, change, glasses on and drive home. Meanwhile, his phone kept buzzing incessantly.

Pulling into the driveway, he glanced at his phone to find a flood of messages from Suzy, complete with photos of her.

'You left in a hurry. Will I see you tomorrow? xxx,' read the last message. Despite his smile, a sense of fear lingered within him. As he sat down for dinner, his mind was a blur. He later climbed into bed and an unusual feeling washed over him. Tonight, he was filled with desire, a burning passion. The intense feeling was driving him insane.

Becks approached the bed, gently massaging moisturiser onto her hands and arms before joining him under the covers. As she lovingly approached her husband and gave him his customary goodnight kiss, an electrifying energy coursed through him. She turned her back and began to place her head on her pillow, when he suddenly pulled her close, kissing her aggressively, and forcing his tongue deep into her mouth. He then pushed her down while laying his weight on her side.

"What are you doing?" she questioned.

"Just kiss me," he demanded firmly. He climbed on top of her, raised her nightgown, removed her underwear, and initiated penetration. She exhaled deeply, bringing her knees towards her ears as he pushed her legs back. Feeling him penetrate deeply she let out a light high-pitched groan. She relished the sensation of his body against hers. As he withdrew from her, he rapidly turned her around and positioned her on all fours, gripping her front to raise her hips in the air. With Suzy's image lingering in his mind, his desire intensified. Thrusting in and out, he quickened his pace, the wet sounds fuelling his arousal. Gripping her hair tightly around his fist, he synchronised the motion of his hand with each forceful thrust.

"Connor!" Becks said loudly,

"Yes! Yes! I know you want this," Connor said, as his head tipped backwards, his eyes closed.

"Connor, Connor, stop!" Becks said repeatedly.

"It's OK, I've got you, that feels so good," he said.

"OW, CONNOR, STOP!" Becks shouted in a loud, high-pitched voice. Suddenly, he snapped back to reality and abruptly halted in his tracks. His gaze shifted downwards, landing on her, before diverting to his hand. There, he discovered a tight grip on a handful of golden locks, a result of his forceful yank.

"Shit! Becks, I'm so sorry," he said. His expression betrayed a sense of deep mortification as he realised the gravity of his actions.

"What was that? Bloody hell!" Becks shouted, as she got up abruptly, grabbed her night dress off the floor and walked to the bathroom.

"I don't know what I was doing, I just got lost in you. I'm so sorry," he said as he followed her.

"Don't follow me, for God's sake!" Becks said, as she slammed the bathroom door shut. He turned back around, put on his bottoms and returned to the bed. Sitting up, he eagerly anticipated her return, meticulously smoothing the sheets. A wave of uncertainty washed over him.

"What on earth am I doing?" he said quietly to himself, placing his face in his hands.

Perched on the toilet seat, Becks couldn't help but think about what had just occurred, before rising to inspect her reflection in the mirror. Feeling the unruly tuft of hair at the back of her head, she swiftly tamed it with a wet hairbrush. After splashing her face with cold water and drying it with a hand towel, she applied face cream and gently massaged it under her eyes. Composing herself, she ran her fingers through her hair and finally opened the bathroom door.

"Are you OK?" he asked in a concerned voice.

"Yes, I'm fine. What happened?" she asked, as she perched on the side of the bed.

"I don't know, I can't explain it," he replied.

"Can I ask you something?" Becks said quietly.

"Yes, of course," he replied in panic.

"Are you taking some kind of steroid for your workout?" she asked.

"No! God, no! I would never do that," Connor replied, feeling a sense of relief.

"Please, let's not repeat that, alright? I enjoy a little excitement but, please, be present," she expressed, as she climbed back into bed. She rolled over, this time without kissing him, switched off her bedside lamp and drifted off to sleep. Connor lay a gentle kiss on her right shoulder, feeling both frustrated and ashamed, before lying down on his back.

The following day, he woke up to once more find the bed empty with Becks' hair still discarded in the waste bin beside the wardrobe. Sitting up, he rubbed his face, put on his glasses, and checked his phone. There were two additional messages from Suzy. Rising his tired body from the bed, he disregarded the messages, took a shower, dressed himself in his shirt and tie, and went downstairs to see his family sitting at the kitchen table. He bid farewell to the boys and Becks, giving her kiss on the cheek and feeling unsure of what to say to her. He was consumed by shame.

"Breakfast?" Becks inquired.

"No, I'll grab a protein bar on my way out. Thank you though," he replied hastily before leaving.

Upon reaching the office, his phone incessantly beeped throughout the morning, yet he chose to ignore it. Later that day, he drove directly home after work, skipping the gym altogether. He sent a message to Becks asking her not to prepare any food – he felt he had some making up to do. As he entered the kitchen, he carried a bouquet and a takeaway. The boys excitedly gathered around him, their energy palpable, while he carefully set the pizza on the kitchen counter.

"Hi, these are for you. I'm sorry," Connor said to Becks, gently kissing her on the cheek and handing her the flowers.

"Thank you, they're beautiful," she said, as she placed her right hand on his cheek and smiled. The family gathered around the dinner table, sharing laughs and stories as they enjoyed their meal together.

Becks tucked the boys into bed, and when Connor found her getting ready for bed, he lovingly asked, "Are you OK?"

"Yes, I'm just exhausted, I'm going to get an early night," Becks replied.

"OK, I have a couple of emails to answer, then I'll be up," he said.

Downstairs, Connor quickly tidied up some leftover dirty glasses, took out the rubbish, and paused in the kitchen. His phone had been buzzing non-stop in his pocket, so he settled on the couch with a beer and noticed a dozen messages from Suzy.

'I missed you tonight, have I done something to upset you? I'm so sorry if I've said something wrong. Will you be at the gym tomorrow? I can't stop thinking about you, thoughts of you are turning me on. Here's something to keep you going,' followed by four pictures, two of her breasts, one of her face, and one of her touching herself intimately. The tightness in his gut was overwhelming, this woman was crazy, but he craved that passion once more. Glancing around to ensure he was alone, he propped his phone against a decorative ornament on the coffee table. Opening the images of Suzy, he began pleasuring himself, vigorously rubbing himself with increasing intensity, unable to resist the urge. Suppressing his moans, he yearned for that exhilaration, all he wanted was to indulge in pure desire. As he ejaculated, he felt a sense of satisfaction, he'd released his tension, and emitted a deep sigh of relief. He tidied up the aftermath on his hands using a tissue from the elegant box resting on the coffee table.

Retrieving his phone, he erased every trace of the messages and pictures. However, unbeknownst to him, Becks stood silently at the foot of the staircase observing his every action and hearing every sound of his pleasure. With only a view of the back of his head, she was astounded as she witnessed him engage in self-pleasure. Straining her eyes, she attempted to catch a glimpse of what had captivated his attention, but his body obstructed her view. Motionless, she carefully avoided the creaky floorboards, frozen in shock as she witnessed her husband abusing himself like a troubled adolescent. After he finished, she silently retreated upstairs and slipped back into bed. In a matter of minutes, he re-entered their bedroom. She instinctively shut her eyes tightly, feigning sleep. He proceeded to the ensuite, used the toilet, washed his hands, and slipped into bed beside his wife, acting as though nothing had occurred. Administering a gentle kiss on her right shoulder, she remained still, overwhelmed by a mix of bewilderment, disappointment, and a sense of betrayal.

Becks woke up the next morning feeling restless, having barely slept. She quietly tiptoed to Connor's side of the bed, where she noticed his phone displaying a stunning family portrait of the four of them as the screensaver. As she admired the picture his alarm blared, startling her. She jumped and, in a rush, quickly placed the phone back where she found it as Connor began to stir. He sat up abruptly.

"Good morning, are you OK?" he asked.

"Yes, just turning off your alarm, you were fast asleep," she replied, as she walked over to the other side of the bedroom. In a rush, he snatched his phone, hoping for an empty inbox. To his relief, there were no messages. As they followed their usual morning routine and headed to work, Becks settled at her desk. Thoughts of what she'd witnessed and Connor's actions from the past two nights consumed her mind. It was haunting, her thoughts racing endlessly. She couldn't help but wonder, it wasn't the fact that he casually pleasured himself, after all, he was a man, but why now? She couldn't understand why he'd been so rough with her. Was he not satisfied? Why didn't he attempt to try again? She wondered what had caught his attention, what had aroused him so intensely. With all these unanswered questions, her thoughts were tormenting her.

After school ended that afternoon, Becks found herself sitting at her desk lost in thought, absentmindedly twirling her pen between her fingers. Suddenly, snapping out of her reverie, she realised she needed to take action. Trying to reach Connor, she called him but, getting no response, she left a voicemail instead.

"Hi, hope you've had a good day. I just called to see how you are. Do you mind coming home straight after work? Please don't go to the gym tonight, I think we need some time together. I'm going to book the babysitter for tomorrow night, too. We should go out. It's Friday night, date night, I think it will do us good. Anyway, call me back once you get this. I love you. Bye," Becks said nervously, as she put the phone back down on the desk.

After picking up the boys from the aftercare club, she drove back home, expecting a call from Connor. However, as the silence persisted, she grew concerned and tried reaching out to him three more times, to no avail. As 6 pm approached, anxiety crept in, prompting her to call his office, only to be met with more unanswered calls.

Seated at the kitchen table, she moved the food she'd meticulously cooked for over an hour around her plate with her fork. Wearing his favourite dress in an attempt to light a spark, she was surrounded by flickering candles and a perfectly set romantic dinner, she wondered what had gone wrong. At 6:10 pm, her phone rang with an unfamiliar landline number. She was startled.

"Hello," she answered.

"Hi, it's me," Connor replied, as music drowned the sound in the background.

"Where are you? I can hardly hear you. I've been worried sick," Becks said sternly.

"So sorry, love, I left my phone at work and didn't realise until I got here. I'm at the gym, I'll only be about an hour, see you soon," Connor replied quickly, and put the phone down.

"OK, please don't be long," she said, but the line had already gone dead. She was suspicious, so she called the number back and, of course, her paranoia proved her wrong.

"Good evening, Total Workout, Justin speaking," the man at the end of the phone answered.

"Sorry, I've dialled the wrong number," Becks said, as she put the phone down rapidly. She stood up, scraped her leftover food into the bin, composed herself, and went upstairs to her boys.

"Boys, it's reading time. Bath, and PJ's on, please," she said, as she smiled at them.

"Mummy, why are you dressed like that?" Logan asked.

"Oh, I just wanted to feel nice. Sometimes Mummy wants to feel good about herself, that's why sweetheart," she replied lovingly.

"You look beautiful Mummy," Rory said, as he smiled.

"Thank you, that's very sweet of you to say," Becks replied, rubbing her fingers through his hair.

While Becks was busy reading bedtime stories and tucking their children into bed, Connor was diligently following his workout routine. He completed his session on the bike and glanced around for Suzy, but she wasn't there. He then moved on to the rowing machine. With each pull of the rope, he channelled his frustration until he finished his final rep. He looked up to see her standing by the weights surrounded by three men vying for her attention, much to his irritation. Their eyes met, and he exhaled deeply, wiping the sweat off his brow as he looked away. She walked towards him.

"Hey," she said.

"Hi," he replied, smiling through the sweaty hair hanging down over his eyes.

"Right, I better go, see you," he said walking away, leaving her standing by the rowing machine. Entering the changing room, he grabbed his towel and shower gel before stepping into the shower stall. Locking the door behind him, he turned on the water, discarded his sweaty t-shirt and shorts into the corner, placed his towel over the cubicle door, and began washing himself. Lost in thoughts of Suzy, he felt himself becoming aroused, his penis was hard and he was consumed by desire.

As he showered, the door clicked open. She'd skilfully manipulated the lock with a coin, entered the shower cubicle, and secured the door behind her. Suddenly, he spun around, revealing his exposed and defenceless state, his emotions laid bare. Her gaze fell upon his erect manhood, prompting a smile to grace her lips. Her gaze fixed upon him and she stood motionless before gradually undressing herself. She discarded her sports bra, peeled off her snug leggings, and slid down her thong. Standing before him, she revealed a flawlessly sculpted and smoothly shaved physique. As he approached her, he pulled her near, their bodies pressed together. Their lips met, and the taste of her tongue was exquisite, reminiscent of sweet pear drops. In a bold move, she pushed him against the wall beneath the shower, dropping to her knees to give him an unforgettable experience of pleasure. The days of receiving oral pleasure in his marriage were a distant memory, but the sensation was exhilarating. Leaning his head back against the wall, water trickled into his mouth, causing him to release a pleasurable groan. His face revealed his ecstasy, unable to be tamed or hidden.

As she rose to her feet, she leaned in for another kiss. However, he scooped her up by her armpits, effortlessly lifting her off the ground. With her legs entwined around his waist, he gently pushed her against the wall, their bodies pressed together in an intimate embrace.

"Are you on the pill?" he whispered, kissing her at the same time.

"Coil," she replied with a deep sigh. He exerted force as he entered her passionately, causing her to release a pleasurable moan. He placed his palm firmly against her lips, silencing her completely as he continued to thrust into her. The muscles in his buttocks tightened, intensifying the sensation. The forceful movements pushed her head against the shower wall, heightening the excitement. As their rhythm increased, she forcefully pressed her nails into his shoulder, leaving behind a mark of her passion and craving. A look of pure contentment decorated her face, leaving no room for anything else.

In that moment of climax they momentarily stopped; their bodies intertwined. He gently released his hand from her mouth and leaned in, their lips meeting as the water cascaded around them. They paused for a few seconds before he lowered her to the ground, his face drenched in water. He spat out the water, took a deep breath, closed his eyes, turned towards the wall, and resumed washing as if the moment had never occurred. After grabbing her clothes, she quickly wrapped herself in a towel and stepped out of the cubicle. Meanwhile, he made his way to the door, ensuring it was securely locked before resuming his shower.

Trembling uncontrollably, his entire body shook with fear as he realised his actions. After washing away the evidence, he emerged from the shower with a towel around his waist. Glancing left and right, he opened the shower door only to find that she'd vanished. After drying himself off, he slipped into his fresh joggers and t-shirt before stepping out through the double doors, clutching his gym bag tightly. Scanning the car park eagerly, he searched for any trace of her presence, but to his disappointment, there was no sign. With a sigh, he tossed his bag into the passenger footwell, settled into the driver's seat, and took a moment to collect his thoughts. Exhaling deeply, he glanced at his reflection through his glasses in the rearview mirror. Closing his eyes momentarily, he shook his head and couldn't help but smirk with satisfaction as he ran his fingers through his hair. With a press of the start button, he shifted the car into drive and swiftly exited the parking space.

Quietly, he made his way back home, his mind filled with flashbacks of the shower. Arriving at 7:45 pm, he entered the house holding his gym bag, only to find his devoted wife in the floral dress that he admired greatly, dinner wrapped in foil warming in the oven, and their children asleep in their beds.

"I'm so sorry, I forgot my phone. I left it on my desk and only realised when I got to the gym. I'm so sorry that I worried you and, look at this, you've gone to so much effort. Goodness, I'm sorry, Becks, if I'd known you'd done all of this..." he said. Without wasting a moment, he wrapped his arms around her and directed his attention towards the table, where the candles stood, their flames extinguished and the wax melted.

"It's OK, I was just worried about you, that's all, no harm done. How was the gym?" she answered sweetly.

"Good, I managed to relieve some tension," he replied. As they sat together, their presence at the table seemed almost routine.

He ate his dinner in silence, their conversation limited, he bore the weight of guilt like a towering mountain.

"If I'd known you'd planned a romantic evening, I would have come straight home. You look beautiful, by the way," Connor said lovingly.

"I called you and left a message asking you to come straight home, but it wasn't meant to be tonight," Becks replied, disappointed. As he polished off his meal, she stood up, swiftly clearing his plate and loading it into the dishwasher. With a flick of a switch, she set the dishwasher in motion, then handed him a refreshing cold beer from the fridge.

"You look like you need this," Becks said, as she placed the beer bottle on the table.

"Thank you," he responded while meeting her gaze, but then he swiftly averted his eyes.

"I'm going to take a shower," Becks said.

"OK, I'll be up shortly," Connor replied awkwardly. He was at a loss when it came to his behaviour around her. His demeanour was tense and rigid, lacking any sense of ease or comfort. Despite his deep love for his wife, they seemed to struggle with being comfortable in each other's presence.

As Becks walked upstairs, she removed her dress and hung it on the wardrobe door before stepping into the shower to clear her mind. Meanwhile, Connor entered the bathroom, tossed his sweaty gym clothes into the laundry basket and stood and urinated.

"Why don't you join me?" Becks asked seductively.

"What, now?" Connor replied, looking over his shoulder.

"Yes, it's been a while since we did this," Becks replied, as she rubbed soap suds all over the top half of her body.

"I'm so tired, love, I just want to lie down," he said, as he shook the remaining urine that was dribbling and washed his hands.

"Connor, please, what's wrong?" she asked.

"Nothing. I'm exhausted, not tonight, please. I want to lie down," he said, walking out of the bathroom. As the water cascaded over her, she couldn't help but wonder what had gone awry.

"He's lost interest in me," she whispered to herself. Stepping out of the shower, Becks wrapped herself in a towel and made her way towards the bed where Connor lay, engrossed in the television.

With an intense stare, she knelt on the bed, discarded her towel, and crawled towards him, locking her eyes with his. As she came close, she pressed herself up against him.

"Kiss me," she said as she rubbed her nose against his.

"Becks," Connor said, abruptly moving his head to the side.

"Kiss me and make love to me. Whatever you want, I'll do it. Just, please, tell me what you want," she said to him in a soft voice, biting his ear.

"Please, I don't like you speaking like that. I'm exhausted, I haven't got anything to give," he replied.

"Why? Why are you exhausted? I know you're not satisfied and I want to satisfy you, tell me what you want. Do you want this?" she asked, as she went to put her head towards his crotch.

"I want you, just you, us, how we are. You're perfect and beautiful, and you're a great wife and a fantastic mum," Connor said, as he pushed her head back.

"Are you saying no? I don't understand you. Have you ever considered that I don't want to be just a great wife and a great mum? I want us, you, to be satisfied," Becks said, desperately.

"I am satisfied. What more do you want me to say?" he said, his frustration towards her growing.

"I'm throwing myself at you, naked might I add, and you're saying no. Why? What the hell is wrong?" Becks asked with a raised voice.

"I'm not saying no, I'm tired," he replied.

"Yes, tired. Well, perhaps you need to go downstairs and do it yourself!" she said irritably, as she got up off the bed and wrapped her towel back around herself.

"What?" Connor shouted in a horrified manner.

"Yes! I saw you. I saw you last night, pleasuring yourself like a juvenile teenager, watching whatever slutty filth you were watching on your phone," Becks replied in anger.

"I-I was just frustrated. I'm sorry, I have no explanation. I'm mortified that you witnessed that, I feel so embarrassed. I didn't know you were there," he replied, stuttering in haste.

"Yes, well, here I am embarrassing myself in attempts to take that frustration away from you. But I guess you have more fun on your own," she replied, as she put on her nightie.

"Don't feel embarrassed. I'm just tired, that's all, I promise," Connor replied, in an attempt to offer her some comfort.

"I don't understand you. For the past two nights you've become rough with me, and then you're masturbating to God knows what on your phone. So, today, I had some self-reflection, perhaps it's me not fulfilling something for you, some fantasy that you want. Hence why I'm here begging you, making a fool of myself, and talking like a first-class tart which I'm guessing is what you want? That cheap, nasty behaviour, is it turning you on? I obviously haven't got any of that, hence why you're saying no to me," Becks replied emotionally.

"Sweetheart, please," Connor begged.

"Do you have any idea how I feel? I feel unattractive, my body's not the best. I feel old and then, I look at you. You're ageing like a fine whisky because I give you time to work out and keep yourself physically and mentally fit, while I waste away into the depths of my late thirties. I don't have massive boobs or big lips, wear ridiculous amounts of makeup or dress up like a tart. Is that what you want? Do you want me, the mother of your children walking around looking like that?" Becks asked in rage.

She was consumed by her anger and couldn't decipher his desires. All she longed for was his contentment and happiness.

"You're beautiful, you're flawless, you're as close to perfection as they come. I was just stupid, a moment of weakness. I have no words to explain. I never do that – I can't even remember the last time I did that. I was just frustrated and I was rough with you a couple of nights ago, and I felt guilty. I felt awful for hurting you. I didn't want to pressure you, I'm sorry," he replied. Overcome with a heavy sense of guilt, Connor struggled to reconcile his behaviour with the person he believed himself to be, acutely aware that his actions did not align with his true character. Meanwhile, Becks found herself in a state of confusion, hurt, and with a desperate need to salvage her marriage, yet remaining oblivious as to what could have caused the deterioration.

"Well, at least you got your frustration out, good for you," she said, as she got into bed and turned her back towards him.

"I'm sorry, please, come here," he said in a tender voice, desperately attempting to atone for his actions. However, no amount of effort could rectify the inexcusable deed he'd committed, leaving him consumed by an overwhelming sense of guilt. He gently kissed her shoulder and rolled back over to his side of the bed. He lay still, his mind refusing to shut out the thoughts of Suzy. Every time he tried to close his eyes, her image would appear, along with the sound of her heavy breathing, resembling a loud heartbeat. The memory of their actions in the shower lingered in his mind, making him determined to never act that way again. He reassured himself that he would message her the next day to confess that it was all a huge mistake.

On Friday morning, a typically cheerful time in the Jones household, Becks was awake earlier than usual as it was the final day of term. The boys were already in the car, all packed up, before Connor had even stirred from his sleep. Startled by the loud slam from the front door, he jolted awake. He walked slowly down the stairs and found himself in a deserted house. Sitting down in his plaid pyjama bottoms and white t-shirt, with his thick black glasses perched on his nose, he indulged in his usual cereal, sitting quietly and savouring its familiar taste. He slowly walked back upstairs, still tormented by the weight of his conscience and unable to shake off the remorse that lingered within him. He refreshed himself with a shower, dressed, and embarked on his journey to work, his mind still shrouded in a haze.

Upon reaching the office, he exchanged the usual morning pleasantries before heading to his desk, his mobile phone lying there with a drained battery. He quickly plugged it in to charge and, soon enough, the messages started flooding in with a series of notifications. Message after message from Suzy, message after message from Becks, her voicemail asking him not to go to the gym, he placed his head in his hands and thought to himself, if only! He began to type a message to Becks.

'Good morning my dear, I want to apologise for last night, I just listened to your voicemail and I feel terrible for ruining your romantic plans. Dinner out tonight sounds wonderful. I'm looking forward to spending time with you. I love you deeply,' he whispered as he typed. With that, he hit send.

He then opened his social media app, eagerly opened Suzy's alluring messages and started composing his response, talking as he typed.

'Last night was a mistake, it can never be repeated. I'm committed to my wife and I love her dearly. I'm sorry Suzy, but please keep your distance,' said the message. Without hesitation, he hit send, knowing he'd made the right choice. However, Suzy's response came swiftly. He read the message out loud.

'You know, deep down, that's not true!' he read. His respiration grew heavy, he felt consumed by a sense of anxiety and he longed for this woman to leave him alone.

As the day progressed, Suzy bombarded him with six more messages, playfully teasing and charming him, leaving him feeling both intrigued and exasperated. Just before noon, she continued the chase and sent him a photo. The image captured her lying on a large bed, adorned with pristine white sheets. Her knees and thighs were partially revealed, while her hand delicately concealed her most intimate self. He read the message.

'I want you again, here! I'm at the Empress Hotel on Wesley Street, room 321. I'll be waiting. Come and have your lunch, I know you're starving!' he read. Trembling once more, he pondered the idea of confronting her directly, hoping that a face-to-face conversation would finally make her understand his urgent need to resolve their situation and break free from it, right here and now!

He picked up his phone, grabbed his coat and walked into the foyer.

"Margaret, I have to pop out, I'll be about an hour," Connor said to his assistant. Margaret, a sixty-two-year-old woman, was known for her nosiness and desire to be involved in every detail of others' lives. Despite needing to retire, she couldn't let go of her habit of being deeply entrenched in everyone's business.

"Yes, no problem. Going anywhere nice?" Margaret asked.

"Just to meet a potential new client," Connor answered.

"That's strange, to meet someone out of the office. I can have the conference room set up for you if you wish, Mr Jones," Margaret said.

"No, Margaret, thank you. He's a very wealthy client and has asked to meet at his hotel. I won't be too long," Connor replied, making his way to the lifts. Exiting his office building, he briskly made his way to the hotel just ten minutes away. En route he mentally rehearsed the words he would say.

Upon reaching the hotel, he headed directly to the elevators, ascending to the third floor while scanning the room numbers, 302, 313, 319, and so on.

"OK, it's the next door," he said to himself. Standing just outside the door, he inhaled deeply before gently tapping on it. Just as he knocked, a housekeeper wheeled a trolley past, narrowly avoiding a collision.

"Oops, so sorry," he apologised, quickly shifting his body to make way, and adjusting his glasses on his nose. As the door swung open, she appeared in a white towel robe, partially revealing a red lace bra. He entered the room, attempting to divert his attention from her attire.

"Right, I've come here to say my piece and then I'm leaving, Suzy. This has to stop, please. You have to stop messaging me and stop coming to the gym. What happened last night was a huge mistake and it can't happen again. Please, I'm begging you. Please, you need to leave me alone," he said desperately.

"You came all the way here, walked into my hotel room to tell me to stop, and you think I'm going to believe that? More to the point, do you believe that?" she replied seductively.

"Suzy, please, this has moved way too quickly, it's out of control. I love my wife, my children, my life, I can't lose that," he pleaded.

"Who said anything about losing that, Connor? I don't want you to leave your wife. This is a bit of fun, that's all," Suzy replied, as she sauntered over to him with an alluring sway in her step. She took off his glasses and set them down on the side table, causing him to start shaking once more.

"You're shaking. You don't need to be scared, I won't bite," she said in a hushed voice, loosening the knot of her robe. Her perfectly manicured fingers ran through his hair and, guiding his hand to her breast, she leaned in slowly and placed her lips on his.

As if losing all self-control, he instantly clasped her in his arms and fervidly kissed her. The intensity of the moment heightened as he plunged his tongue into her mouth, exploring and teasing, while gently nibbling on her bottom lip. With a quick motion, he tossed her onto the bed. He removed his coat, suit jacket, and tie, and he tore off his shirt, revealing his sculpted chest and abs. Unfastening his belt, he kicked off his shoes and approached her, his gaze locked onto hers, his heart racing. He knelt on the bed, gently removing her underwear and sliding them down her legs. Pulling her closer by her thighs, he began to pleasure her, exploring every inch with his tongue and lips. The intensity grew as she became wet and started to moan passionately. Gripping the bed sheets tightly, she let out a scream of pleasure, her face contorting with ecstasy.

He positioned himself over her, swept his hand through his hair, playfully nibbled on her nipples, lifted her legs, and thrust vigorously, causing her to bite her lip to stifle a scream.

"Turn over. I'm going to fuck you so damn hard!" he said, flipping her over onto her stomach. He positioned himself on top of her, intertwining their fingers above her head as he entered her once more, feeling a newfound intensity he'd never experienced before. She awakened a primal side of him that he never knew existed. With each thrust, her mouth agape, the force expelled the air from her lungs. Beads of sweat trickled down his face as he gasped for breath, and in the moment of release, he shut his eyes, rested his face against the curve of her back and relished in the sheer pleasure of it all.

Gradually, he moved backwards and lay on his back, with only the white sheets concealing his masculinity. Their breathing was laboured. She rested her head on the pillow beside him in silence, no words exchanged between them. Suddenly, his eyelids drooped, and he drifted off into a deep sleep, completely unconscious. Suzy glanced at him and stood up cautiously, ensuring not to disturb him. She wrapped herself in the dressing gown and silenced his phone. She approached his trousers, retrieved his wallet, pulled out his driver's licence, and snapped a photo of the information using her phone. With a mischievous smile, she approached him and captured a snapshot of him peacefully asleep. Silently, she tiptoed across the room, meticulously arranging everything back to its original position. Slipping into her underwear, she made her way to the bathroom where her clothes awaited her. Swiftly getting dressed, she returned to the bedroom, pulling the curtains shut to envelop the room in darkness. Leaving Connor undisturbed, she departed, leaving him to his dreams.

Connor jolted awake after two and a half hours, feeling disorientated and bewildered. He hastily sat up, only to realise that he was all by himself in the dimly lit hotel room, with no trace of Suzy.

"Suzy, Suzy!" he called out, but she was nowhere to be found. Glancing at his phone, he saw the time. It was 3:27 pm and he'd missed eight calls, five from Becks and three from the office. With trembling hands, he dialled Becks' number. As the phone rang, a wave of panic washed over him. In a rush, he gathered his scattered clothes from the floor and hastily slipped into his boxer shorts.

"Connor, where the hell are you?" she said as she picked up the phone. Amidst the noise of passing cars, her voice echoed with a shout.

"Becks, I'm so sorry, I was in a meeting with a new client and I must have clicked my phone onto silent. I didn't hear it, sorry. Are you OK? I have several missed calls from you. Are you in the car?" he asked.

"Yes, yes, we're in the car. It's my dad. He's had a heart attack and is in coronary care. They're not sure if he's going to make it. I'm driving over now with the boys. I tried calling you and I called the office, but Margaret said you were out. Why are you meeting clients outside of the office? For God's sake, I needed you!" she replied, crying down the phone.

"I'm so sorry. I just didn't hear the calls. I'll come now. Turn around and we can drive over together," he replied.

"I'm only thirty minutes away from the hospital now. I think we're going to be here all night; I'll keep you updated. I need to go, there's traffic everywhere and this had to happen on a Friday afternoon!" she said in a state of panic, as she abruptly ended the call.

"FUCK! FUCK!" Connor yelled, slamming his hand on the bedside table. After hastily getting dressed, he washed his face, fixed his hair, double-checked the room, and swiftly exited the hotel.

Hurrying back to the office, he sprinted up the stairs and dashed into the foyer.

"Mr Jones, Rebecca has been on the phone several times asking for you," Margaret said with concern.

"Yes, thank you, Margaret, I've spoken to her. I have to go. I'll be available on the phone if you need anything. I'll see you on Monday," he said, grabbing his laptop bag and work folders. He hurriedly dashed out of the building towards his car. Margaret noticed that he'd left all his work items behind for his supposed meeting. She stood watching him through her glasses as he rushed past in a state of panic.

On his way home, he tried calling Becks once more, but she didn't answer. Upon reaching the house, he hurried upstairs, shed his work attire, washed away the scent of Suzy, brushed his teeth, and changed into jeans and a polo shirt. With two small suitcases in hand, he carefully packed clothes for the boys, Becks, and himself to last the weekend. After grabbing snacks and juices for the boys from the kitchen, he hurried back to the car and embarked on his journey across the country to be reunited with his family.

After enduring a gruelling three hours of traffic, he finally reached the hospital in a state of panic. Unfortunately, he hadn't had the opportunity to speak with Becks again, leaving him clueless about their whereabouts. Desperate for answers, he approached various staff members, but none could provide any information. He checked the Accident and Emergency Department as well as the Intensive Care Unit, but his father-in-law was nowhere to be found, which made him nervous. In a last-ditch effort, he informed a lady at the main reception about the heart attack and was directed to the Coronary Care Unit. With hope in his heart, he made his way to the reception desk, fervently praying that he would find them there.

"Bob, Robert Pritchard, he had a heart attack. My wife Rebecca is with him, are they here on this ward?" he said in a rush.

"Yes, yes sir, your wife is in the relatives' room, third door on your right," the lady replied. With soft steps, he made his way towards the door, taking a moment to steady his breath.

Adjusting his shirt with a touch of finesse, he gently pushed his glasses up his nose before softly tapping on the door.

"Come in," Becks' voice said.

"Daddy!" the boys shouted as they ran to him.

"Hey guys, how is he?" Connor asked, as he placed his arm around his wife's shoulder.

"Not good, his heart stopped. Luckily Jason and Jacob were both there. They did CPR and thankfully managed to restart his heart, he could have died, he could have died," Becks cried. Connor held his wife tightly, his arms strong and comforting. His heart was beating rapidly, but he was relieved to be by her side at that moment.

"OK, shhh, it's OK, he's in the best place now," Connor said as he stroked her hair. His hands trembled and a lump formed in his throat as he felt overwhelming shame. He clung tightly to his family, realising he'd failed to be the pillar of strength they needed in their time of need.

An hour later in his in-laws' house, which had not been updated since the early 1990s, Connor spent the night away from his own home in the unfamiliar bedroom that once belonged to his wife as a child. With his two boys peacefully sleeping on mattresses beside him, he anxiously scrolled through his social media, eagerly anticipating Becks' arrival. As he continued to scroll, Suzy's messages kept flooding in. It was time to take action. He composed a different response this time, expressing his regret and pleading for her to stop contacting him. After hitting send, he deleted all their previous conversations and blocked her. Thankfully, he hadn't shared his phone number with her, and he hoped that, by cutting off contact on the only social media platform they shared, he could finally put an end to this situation.

Becks made her way to bed, where Connor pulled back the covers. She approached him, tears streaming down her face. He embraced her tightly, gently rubbing her back to comfort her.

"I don't know what I would have done if he hadn't made it, bloody hell, I just…" she said, as she continued to cry.

"OK, sweetheart, he'll be OK, he'll be OK," Connor replied, in an attempt to console her.

"I think we should move. I feel the need to be close to them," Becks suggested as she sobbed.

"Let's just take each day as it comes, OK? This is a huge shock. Why don't you and the boys stay for a week. It's half term anyway, you can be here for your mum and your dad. He may be discharged before you leave later in the week," Connor replied.

"You wouldn't mind that?" Becks asked.

"Of course not, I'll ring the office on Monday and take a couple of days off, and drive back home on Tuesday. If I go to work Wednesday, Thursday, Friday, I can travel back here Friday night, does that sound OK?" Connor replied lovingly.

"Yes, that would be great, thank you. I'm so glad you're here," Becks replied, placing her head on his shoulder.

"I wouldn't want to be anywhere else," he whispered, kissing her head.

The following day, Bob had made it through the night. Despite a restless sleep, Becks and Joan went back to the hospital, while Connor decided to take the boys out for a day filled with enjoyment, hoping to distract them from the distressing circumstances. Upon reaching the hospital, Connor leaned over to kiss Becks, his smile filled with affection. At that moment, he realised the extent of his wrongdoing and the guilt he carried, even though Becks remained unaware of it. Connor treated the boys to a fun day out, starting with bowling, followed by a nice lunch, and a trip to the supermarket for dinner ingredients. Later, they picked up Becks and Joan from the hospital at 6 pm, walking slowly to the ward. Connor couldn't help but feel guilty as he passed by each patient, his conscience weighing heavily on him. The boys ran to Becks.

"Mummy," Logan shouted, as they entered Bob's side room.

"Hi, how is he?" Connor asked quietly.

"You can ask him yourself," Becks replied, smiling.

"Goodness, Bob, you gave us all a fright," Connor said.

"You can't break a good working man down that easily," Bob replied as he coughed.

"Dad, just lay back and rest, please," Becks said, passing him a cup of water and holding his straw as he took a sip.

Following twenty minutes of casual conversation, they departed from the hospital, allowing Bob to recuperate. The boys were in high spirits, singing along in the car and engaging in a game of rock, paper, scissors with Granny Joan seated between them. Connor placed his hand on Becks' leg, feeling a sense of relief and comfort that had been absent for days. He looked at Becks and smiled.

"Thank you for being here," Becks said, as she smiled at him and squeezed his hand.

"I'm here for you, for all of you," he said, while trying to hold back his inner guilt.

As the night fell, Connor found himself lying in bed once more, feeling the uncomfortable springs of the worn out mattress pressing against his back. The boys, filled with excitement, were also nestled on their mattresses, relishing in the thrill of the adventure. Suddenly, Becks entered the room, clad in her loose-fitting pyjamas, her hair tied up in a scrunchy atop her head. Standing at the doorway, she met Connor's gaze, prompting a warm smile to spread across his face.

"Not very sexy," Becks said, as she pulled on the bottom of the long-sleeved t-shirt.

"You look amazing in anything you wear, you're beautiful," Connor replied, looking in awe at his wife. Becks approached the bed, climbed onto the unstable mattress, and settled next to her husband. They then shifted positions, now facing each other.

"I'm so relieved, what a few days!" Becks expressed quietly.

"I know, I'm glad he's OK. He needs to slow down Becks," Connor said.

"I know. I'll speak to him once he gets home. Thank you for today, and your support. It means everything to just have you here, especially when I know how much you hate not having an ensuite," Becks said as she laughed.

"I'll walk down the hall to take a pee for you any day, Mrs Jones," he said, gazing at her.

Gently, she caressed his cheek with her left hand before planting a soft kiss on his lips, her touch as gentle as a delicate flower. This was what he truly desired, not the vulgar behaviour that had turned his head. As they kissed, Connor drew closer, and they both fidgeted to shed their pyjama bottoms and unite their naked lower halves beneath the covers.

"Bloody hell, I feel like a teenager again," Becks said, laughing.

"And how many boys did you have in this house as a teenager?" Connor asked sarcastically.

"Good point!" Becks said, as she climbed on top of him, leaned forward and pulled the covers over her head. As they engaged in intimacy, the springs beneath them creaked, but they were too lost in each other to care, sharing tender moments of love. Afterwards, Becks lay on his chest, legs intertwined, feeling a deep connection she hadn't felt in months. Connor held her close, his head resting against hers, both content in the silence and closeness they shared.

After ten minutes, Connor whispered, "Are you asleep?"

"No, I'm just enjoying this," Becks replied.

"Me too, me too," he said softly, as he continued embracing her.

"I do think I need to move though," Becks said as she sat up.

"Don't move, please," Connor replied.

Becks rose from her reclined position, her legs firmly positioned on either side of his waist. The moon's radiant glow seeped through the thin curtains, casting an ethereal light on her exposed form.

"We need to do better, we must make time for each other, as a family, and as a couple. I don't want to lose this, lose us," Becks said.

"You'll never lose me, I love you, I love us, you're all I've ever wanted and still want, Becks. I'm sorry," Connor replied.

"What for?" Becks asked.

"Everything. I haven't conducted myself well at all over the past few weeks. I'll try harder and I'll be better, for all of you," Connor said. Becks remained seated on him as he sat up. He kissed her lips, before resting his head on her chest.

"I love you," he whispered. Becks reciprocated the sentiment with a deep breath, then peeled herself away from him,

"I'm literally stuck to you!" Becks said, as she took a tissue from the box on the side of the bed and wiped her inner thigh.

"Here," she said, passing a handful of tissues to Connor.

"I think I'll tiptoe down the hall and clean myself up. This is why we have an ensuite," he said, as he playfully tiptoed out of the bedroom, giggling.

He stood up from the bed, slipped into his pyjama bottoms and made his way to the bathroom with hushed steps. After lifting the toilet seat, he relieved himself while stretching his neck from side to side. He exhaled deeply, shook off the remaining drops, and cleaned up with a tissue. Making his way to the sink, he cleansed his hands and gazed at his reflection in the mirror. Leaning against the sink, he paused, fixating on his image, his grip on the sink tightening. Refreshing his face with a splash of cold water, he brushed his teeth before returning to the bedroom.

As he re-entered the room, he found Becks and his adorable boys fast asleep. Rory's hand dangled over the edge of the bed, prompting him to gently tuck it back in. He gave a tender kiss on Rory's head before settling down beside Becks. Lying on his side, he watched her sleep peacefully, his mind filled with remorse.

How could I have caused such pain to her and our children? he thought. Despite his determination and strength, he couldn't escape the overwhelming guilt that would forever linger within him.

By Tuesday, Bob showed significant improvement and was able to walk around, although he easily grew fatigued. Becks decided to stay back as planned, to assist her mother and enjoy some quality time together. After a lengthy journey, Connor finally reached his house and parked his car. His surroundings were cold, dark and wet. He stood in the hallway and, feeling the absence of his loved ones, unpacked his suitcase, took a shower, and prepared a sandwich. Sitting at the kitchen table, he reflected on his gratitude for them and the emptiness of the unusually quiet house. As the clock struck 10:30 pm, he settled into his cosy bed. Although empty, he couldn't help but appreciate the luxurious comfort of his bed, especially when compared to the worn out mattress at his in-laws' house.

Glancing at his phone for a moment of relaxation, an unexpected knock suddenly echoed through the silence, causing him to question the identity of the visitor.

"Who could be at the front door at such an hour?" he said to himself, his curiosity piqued. With a twist of the handle, he was met with a sight that took him by surprise. There she was, the alluring seductress he believed was a distant memory.

"Hi," Suzy said in a high-pitched voice.

"Jesus Christ, Suzy, what the hell are you doing here?" he said, as he grabbed her by the forearm and pulled her inside.

"Ooh, forceful," Suzy said, letting out a small laugh.

"Why are you here and how do you know where I live?" he asked. She remained motionless, gazing at him in silence while her hood shielded her face, raindrops falling onto the floor. A moment of pause.

"Well? Listen, I don't even care, you have to go, you have to go, now," he said again in a masterful voice.

"Why? I know she isn't here. Becks, right?" she asked. Connor was taken aback. How did this woman know so much information?

"Suzy, please, you have to go, please. Just leave me alone, what happened was wrong, it was wrong. Please, I beg you," he pleaded.

"Will you relax. I don't want a relationship with you, it's a bit of fun, lighten up, you can be such a stiff," she replied, as she took her hood down and started to wander around looking at the family pictures that hung on the walls. "Nice house, very cute," she said sarcastically.

"Suzy, what do you want from me?" Connor asked.

"I think you know what I want," she said, as she began to unzip her coat, revealing only a bra underneath. She unbuttoned her tight jeans, and slowly peeled them off, standing in her underwear.

"No, no, I'm sorry, I can't. This was a huge mistake – I can't repeat it. Please, put your trousers and your coat back on, and go," he said, as he gathered her garments from the ground and pressed them firmly against her. She clung onto him tightly, wrapping her arms around his neck.

"Come on. You want it, I want it," she whispered, as she gently touched his lips with hers. Once more he found himself without any control.

"Please, I can't do this," he said quietly.

"You can. It feels good, you know it does," she seductively whispered in his ear, as her hand rubbed over the top of his trousers to feel his semi-erect penis.

His breath quickened as he surged forward, embracing her with enthusiastic kisses, lifting her effortlessly and carrying her to the couch. He lay on top of her as she clung to him, their lips locked in a passionate embrace. His hand slipped inside her underwear, initiating her pleasure. Yet, with a sense of realisation, a feeling of unease crept over him.

"Stop. Stop, Suzy, STOP!" he shouted, as he pulled out of her grip and stood up.

"Just enjoy this for what it is, one last time, then I'll leave you alone, I promise," she said. As she lay with her legs spread, she began rubbing her right index finger over the crotch of her knickers.

"One more time, then you promise to leave me alone?" he asked.

"Just one more, you know you want to," Suzy replied. She confidently rose from where she lay and stood in front of him once again. She unhooked the clasp of her bra from behind and slowly removed her pants, her seductive skills were flawless. She walked towards him, her eyes locked on his, and pushed him onto the sofa chair, the very one he'd used while pleasuring himself to her image not so long ago. She dropped to her knees and crawled towards him, slowly removing his chequered pyjama bottoms. She proceeded to pleasure him, expertly combining sucking with sensual thigh caresses. Resting his head on the sofa, he released a heavy sigh. Without a thought, she stood up and straddled him. With her thighs resting on either side of his, she slipped him inside of her, a perfect fit.

Moving in unison he caressed her back and pleasured her nipples, the passion undeniable and intense. The moment felt forbidden yet undeniably perfect. A pleasurable sigh escaped her lips as she reached the peak of ecstasy. Overwhelmed by desire, he climaxed swiftly, trembling and gasping for air as he rested his head on her pert chest. However, he suddenly came to his senses and soon realised how wrong this was, leaving him feeling empty and ashamed as he opened his eyes to the reality of the situation.

"OK! You have to go, Suzy, please, you've got to go," he said abruptly, as he stood up out of the chair and pushed her from him rapidly.

"Connor," Suzy said, with a displeased demeanour and a grimaced expression, as he moved her off of him. He put his pyjama bottoms back on and handed her clothes to her.

"That was the last time Suzy. I mean it, please, just leave, don't message me, don't come here again and stay away from the gym. I have to give my marriage and my children all of my attention, do you understand?" he said desperately. Standing in his chequered pyjama bottoms he gave off a vulnerable appearance.

"Let's see if you can stay away," she replied, leaning down to slip on her underwear and revealing the uncovered space between her legs. He quickly averted his gaze when she caught him looking, only to meet her cheeky smile as she turned back around.

Annoyingly, she slowly lowered herself onto the chair before slipping into her jeans and coat. He strode towards the front door, leaving her behind. Looking back at her slowly walking towards him, he was becoming irritated.

"Don't push me," he said, as he held the door open and stood tall. As she exited, she brushed passed him and pulled up her hood, prompting him to shut his eyes and lower his head. He then closed the door behind her, observing her stride across the street from the tiny window before she hopped into her black car and drove away.

Returning to the sofa in just his bottoms, he grabbed his t-shirt from the ground and his glasses from the coffee table. He fluffed the cushions and spotted a damp mark on the chair as he made his way over.

"For fuck's sake!" he muttered to himself. He walked briskly to the kitchen and reached for a spray tucked away beneath the sink before starting to scrub the stain vigorously. He sprayed air freshener generously on the sofas, determined to eliminate any lingering traces of her scent. He walked upstairs only to realise he'd missed two calls from Becks.

"Shit!" he said to himself. Despite his repeated attempts, she didn't answer when he called her back. In frustration, he resorted to leaving a voicemail, spewing a stream of lies without a hint of hesitation.

"Hi love, I'm so sorry, I was in the shower when you called, I hope everything's OK. I miss you guys and I can't wait to see you on Friday night. I was thinking, I'll get the train over to you so we can drive home together on Sunday. I'm going to bed now, I love you very much, speak tomorrow. Goodnight, love," he said.

His words flowed fluently – he'd mastered the art of deception and the lies spilt from his lips effortlessly. Once more, he stepped into the shower, scrubbing himself clean, yet her image haunted him every time he shut his eyes. Frustrated, he clenched his fists and placed them against the shower tiles. As the water fell over his head, he pondered the disappointment he felt in himself. After turning off the water, he wrapped a towel around his waist, retrieved fresh pyjamas from the drawer, and climbed into his empty marital bed.

In the days that followed, Connor resumed his usual work routine, making sure to keep his social media app deleted in hopes of avoiding any further encounters with Suzy. He focused on work, avoided the gym, and made sure to FaceTime Becks and the boys twice daily. He felt rejuvenated and determined, with a clear purpose in mind to prioritise his family and, finally, let go of Suzy. It was clear to him that he had to overcome this obstacle and strive to be a supportive figure for his family.

During her half term break, Becks stayed at her parents' home, taking care of paperwork, visiting Bob in the hospital, and enjoying quality time with her mum. For the first time in a long time, she appreciated the peacefulness of the countryside and the presence of her family. Embracing the farming lifestyle once again, she found solace in long walks amidst the crisp air, relishing the taste of home-grown vegetables, and savouring the delightful aromas of the outdoors. To ensure their hard-working and famished bellies were satisfied by day's end, she lovingly prepared slow-cooked meals that started simmering at 9 am. As they walked through the door, the aroma of the freshly prepared meal filled their nostrils, instantly filling their hearts with a deep sense of contentment and appreciation.

After tucking the boys in bed on Wednesday evening, Becks headed to her mother's room. Joan, who had just showered, was wearing the mint green fluffy dressing gown Becks had gifted her for Christmas that year. Sitting at her nineteen seventies-style wooden dressing table, Joan looked at herself in the mirror.

"Are you OK, Mum?" Becks asked, standing at her mother's bedroom door.

"Yes, just wondering how I became this old," Joan replied with a smile.

"It's catching up on us all," Becks replied.

"So it is," Joan said.

"Here, Mum, let me do your hair for you," Becks requested.

"That would be lovely, I don't usually get time to sit like this, not when your father is here," Joan said, with a hint of sadness on her face. Becks held her perspectives on her father's treatment of her mother, yet she chose to keep her thoughts to herself.

Right now, she simply wanted to savour this precious moment with her mum, a luxury that had become increasingly scarce in her life. Becks gently styled her mother's hair, using the blow dryer to achieve a sleek, straight look. As she admired her mother's joyful expression in the mirror, she felt a sense of fulfilment in being able to pamper her and make her feel special. Gazing into the mirror, Joan's eyes met her daughter's reflection. Inhaling deeply, she couldn't help but beam with affection for her beloved child.

"Thank you, dear, that looks much better," Joan said, as she looked at Becks in the mirror, smiling warmly.

Despite its age, the house brimmed with memories she'd long ignored, believing they hindered her progress. Becks was overwhelmed with nostalgia, reminiscing about her childhood and teenage years. However, this time a wave of happiness washed over her, breaking the long spell of melancholy that had clouded her mind. The laughter and happiness surrounding her made her reflect on her own life. Had all her actions been a grave error? After two decades of absence, it wasn't until her father's near-death experience that she returned home and recognised the peaceful childhood she'd been lucky to experience.

Becks would start her day by sitting in the conservatory with her laptop, a cosy blanket draped over her legs, and an electric heater keeping her warm. From there, she would observe her brothers playing with Rory and Logan, getting covered in mud but radiating pure joy. Luckily, the boys found excitement in assisting on the farm and were warmly welcomed by Beck's two brothers. Jacob and Jason, two bachelors deeply devoted to their family farm, remained unmarried and childless despite now being in their thirties. Even though Jason was in a relationship with Julie, a horse enthusiast who lived nearby, the brothers showed no intention of starting families of their own anytime soon.

As the sun began to set on Thursday evening, the chilly air enveloped the surroundings. As Becks entered the kitchen, her eyes were drawn to the familiar sight of the wooden placemats neatly stacked in the middle of the table. These placemats held a sentimental charm from her childhood, evoking both a sense of comfort and disdain. Becks had always despised any form of clutter on her kitchen table, ensuring that everything had its designated spot in her home. However, the presence of these placemats now brought her an unexpected solace, leaving her deep in thought about the reasons behind her current dissatisfaction with her own life.

Becks went on to prepare a hearty beef stew in the slow cooker, along with a generous serving of mashed potatoes and

Yorkshire puddings. She eagerly awaited the moment to gather around the table with her family and savour the delicious meal she'd lovingly prepared.

"Wow, this looks great, Becks. I'm famished!" Jacob exclaimed, signalling his hunger.

"Thanks to all the home-grown veg, you really can live off this farm," she said energetically.

"You certainly can, isn't that right boys? Did you tell Mummy? They learnt how to milk a cow today," Jacob replied.

"Really? That's super, well done boys," Becks said, her face radiating with genuine affection

"Yeah, and when Rory did it, it squirted in his face," Logan said laughing. "It went up my nose and made me sneeze, Mummy," Rory said as he laughed.

Becks' brothers couldn't have been more different from her. Education held no appeal for them, as their entire existence revolved solely around the farm. Jason, a towering man with rugged good looks and a generous heart, maintained a clean-shaven appearance and sported braces atop his work attire. Being at school was a constant struggle for him, labelled as simple, he had a late growth spurt and endured bullying as a skinny child. Expressing emotions was tough for him, however, he always found solace in Jacob's support, hence their closeness. Despite his hands and nails being constantly dirty, he managed to always smell fresh and kept his hair neatly trimmed.

In contrast, Jacob possessed a sharp intellect, displayed impeccable grooming, and despite being smaller than Jason, boasted a robust upper physique. Excelling academically, he also excelled in sports and enjoyed popularity in his school days, yet he never aspired to surpass any lofty ambitions. Jason was known for his straightforwardness, never holding back his thoughts. In contrast, Jacob was more introverted, preferring to observe from the sidelines.

Becks leaned in, serving stew and mash to the boys at the table. She settled back, ready to eat, when her mum gently touched her hand so tenderly.

"Thank you for being here. I'm going to miss you when you go on Sunday," Joan said, smiling lovingly.

"I've loved it, Mum," Becks replied with a smile.

"So, Grandad's coming home tomorrow, are you excited boys?" Jason asked.

"Yes, but then we have to go home. Isn't that right, Mummy?" Logan asked.

"Yes, you guys have school on Monday, and we can't miss school," Becks replied.

"I don't want to go home, I like it here," Rory said, as he scooped a fork full of mash and put it in his mouth.

The room fell quiet as everyone dug into their meals, savouring each bite in silence.

"So, Jason, when are you going to pop the question to Julie?" Becks asked randomly.

"Jesus, where did that come from?" Jason replied, spluttering.

"Well, I've spent some time with her this week and she's lovely. You don't want that one getting away," Becks replied.

"We're just seeing how it goes; I have a lot going on right now with the farm and she's busy, too," Jason replied confidently.

"You're not getting any younger and you need some little people ready to take over," Becks said, as she looked at her brother.

"Yeah, I guess you're right, I don't know, we haven't spoken about it. What do you think, Mum?" Jason asked.

"Yes, I think it would be wonderful and just what the family needs after your dad. Julie is lovely, she's so patient and kind," Joan replied positively. Jason sat deep in thought.

"I think we're just happy plodding along, she hasn't mentioned anything," Jason replied.

"Why would she? That's your job. How old is she?" Becks asked.

"She's thirty-one, but she's always seemed happy with how things are," Jason added.

"Well, what are you waiting for?" Becks asked.

"I don't know," Jason responded.

"Do you know what? Your father has your grandmother's ring upstairs. I think if we give it a polish and a clean, she would like it," Joan said.

"Really? Do you think Dad would be OK with that?" Jason asked.

"I think he would be very proud. I'll get it out after dinner and you can ask him tomorrow," Joan replied.

Becks beamed with satisfaction as she observed everyone eagerly devouring the meal she'd lovingly cooked. In addition to relishing this moment, she yearned to reconnect with her family, and what could be a more perfect opportunity than taking charge of a Pritchard wedding? The Pritchard family members' lives were incredibly modest lives that, if she were being truthful, she now regarded with aversion. They lacked the glamour of a high-flying lifestyle, urban education, or the financial prosperity of a higher tax bracket. At this moment, she found herself questioning what she'd transformed into.

Once dinner was over, she bathed the boys and dressed them in fresh pyjamas. Ever since Connor had left, she'd been sleeping in the middle of them at night, cherishing the warmth of their togetherness in one bed. It was a feeling she'd longed for. After tucking them in and giving them goodnight kisses, she quietly made her way down the hallway to her mother's room.

"Are you OK, Mum?" Becks asked.

"Yes, I'm just going through this jewellery box to find your grandmother's ring. These were my mother's pearls, and my grandmother's broach," Joan said, as she held them up and looked at them with admiration.

"They're beautiful, Mum," Becks said.

"Here, you take them," Joan said.

"No, Mum, you keep hold of them," Becks replied.

"They'll come to you when I die anyway, so you may as well, or maybe they're not expensive enough," Joan said, as she clutched them in her hands.

"No, no, Mum, they're priceless heirlooms, it's not about expense. Is that what you think of me?" Becks asked.

"No, sweetheart, I just know you have different tastes now, that's all," Joan replied calmly.

"Mum, I'm still me, I'm still your daughter," Becks replied with concern. Becks despised the idea of her mother having a negative opinion of her, feeling conflicted between her past and current self.

"I know you are. Oh, here it is, your grandmother's engagement ring. Do you know your father's father gave her this ring on her twenty-first birthday? They were married for sixty-three years before he died," Joan said.

"That's beautiful, marriages aren't like that anymore," Becks said.

"Some are, if you put the effort in," Joan said quietly, as she rose to her feet, gently touching Beck's cheek with her right hand before exiting the room and making her way downstairs. As they made their way downstairs, Becks noticed her brothers sprawled across the sofas, completely absorbed in the TV.

"Mum's found the ring," Becks said, as she perched on the arm of the sofa.

"Has she? Yeah, let's have a look," Jason said.

"She's cleaning it in the kitchen," Becks replied. Jason stood up and Becks followed him to the kitchen.

"It's coming up like a new penny, look how shiny that is now," Joan exclaimed with joy, as she raised it towards the light, watching it sparkle.

"It's nice, Mum, thank you. I'll ask Dad tomorrow," Jason said. Becks sensed her gradual return to the inner circle and a feeling of contentment washed over her.

Becks woke up bright and early on Friday morning. She decided to take her boys out to the farm and asked her brothers to keep an eye on them. Afterwards, she hopped into her car and embarked on a seven-mile journey to the town centre. It had been ages since she last visited this town but, to her surprise, not much had changed. While some shops had closed down, Petersons, the renowned jeweller on the corner, was still standing strong. Being the only jeweller in town, they offered a wide range of services, from replacing watch batteries, to repairing broken chains, and even crafting new jewellery pieces.

After parking her car, she strolled across the road and gazed through the shop window at the modest displays, prompting her to reflect on her journey, from a small-town girl to successful urban high-flyer, and contemplate the incredible path she'd taken. The absence of luxury brands in the shop made her realise how much she'd evolved, as the old-fashioned and outdated jewellery stood in stark contrast to the high-street fashion she now embraced. As she entered the store, the familiar sound of the bell echoed through the room, instantly transporting her back to 2001.

"Good morning, I'm looking for a ring box. Do you sell the boxes on their own?" Becks asked.

"Yes, yes we do. Special occasion, is it?" asked Graham, the jeweller. Graham, a mature man in his sixties, sported a head of thick grey hair and was impeccably dressed in a shirt and tie.

"I hope so. My brother is proposing to his girlfriend with my grandmother's ring and I want to surprise him. I have the ring here. Is it possible for you to give it a clean and box it up for him?" she asked.

"Well, that is a fine piece. Goodness, this must be at least a hundred years old, they don't make them like this anymore. No problem, my dear, I'll just go into the back and give it a polish, and find you a nice box," he said.

Becks was pleasantly reminded of the warmth and kindness that small-town residents exuded when engaging in conversation. Each interaction during her visit filled her heart with joy and nostalgia.

"Thank you, that's very kind of you," Becks replied, as Graham disappeared out back.

"Are you not from around here, my dear?" Graham asked loudly, as the machine began to generate noise.

"I used to be. Haven't lived here for a long time," she replied.

"Oh. What brings you back?" Graham asked, as he walked back to the counter, vigorously polishing the ring with his cloth.

"My dad. You might know him – Bob Pritchard? He's been unwell, so I've come home for a week to help my mum," Becks replied.

"Well, I never, are you Rebecca?" Graham asked.

"Yes, yes that's me," Becks replied, smiling.

"My goodness, I haven't seen you since you were, well, I dread to think how long it's been," Graham said.

"You know my mum and dad?" Becks asked.

"Of course, who doesn't? How is your dad?" Graham asked.

"He's being discharged this afternoon. He had a heart attack, but, thankfully, he's doing well now," Becks replied.

"Great to hear. Well, it's lovely to see you, my goodness, how time flies. Right, how does that look? It's polished up like a shiny new penny. Will this box do?" he asked, as he placed it in a black velvet ring box.

"That looks beautiful, thank you. How much do I owe you?" Becks asked, as she reached inside her handbag for her purse.

"Nothing, this is on me. Tell Jason, good luck, and mum's the word," Graham said, as he winked and tapped his nose.

"How did you know it was Jason?" Becks asked.

"Well, Julie is my niece," Graham replied.

"Oh, please don't say anything," Becks asked in a panic.

"Not a word. I look forward to seeing you at the wedding. Give your dad my love," Graham said.

"I will. Sorry, what was your name?" Becks asked.

"Graham. He'll know," Graham answered.

"Thank you, Graham, it was a pleasure to meet you," Becks replied, with a look of delight on her face. Becks grinned as she strolled out, a sense of warmth came over her. The town exuded a pleasant and wholesome charm that she'd failed to notice or appreciate in her youth.

Becks returned to her childhood home, indulging in the beauty of the surroundings, savouring every moment of the scenic route on her drive home. She parked the car and entered just as everyone was enjoying their morning tea break. Walking into the kitchen with the ring box in hand, she found her family gathered around the wooden table. Resting on the table was a teapot, complete with its cosy, alongside a plate of biscuits and a glass bottle containing milk. Her two boys indulged in chocolate digestives dipped in hot chocolate, a perfect moment captured in time.

"Where have you been so early?" Jason asked.

"I've been to get this done," Becks said, handing him the ring box.

"What's this?" Jason said, as his eyes widened. He opened the box with his large dirty fingers,

"Do you like it?" Becks asked.

"I can't believe you did this; it looks like new, and the box, too. Wow, thank you," Jason said, as he approached her with open arms, planting a warm hug around her tiny frame. Joan sat there, mug in hand, with a smile playing on her lips, reminiscing about the strong bond they once shared, now slowly rekindling.

"When are you going to do it?" Becks asked.

"I'll ask Dad and if he's happy, maybe tonight. She's coming over, so why not," Jason said.

"Are you not going to take her out somewhere special?" Becks asked.

"Why? There's no better place than being at home, surrounded by family. Not everything has to be a huge grand gesture," Jason replied sharply.

"I didn't mean it like that, it sounds lovely, just do me a favour though, put a clean shirt on at least," Becks replied, in an attempt to salvage her previous comment. Jason smiled and gazed at the ring.

"Your father will be thrilled," Joan added.

"Speaking of Dad, I think we should make a move, Mum, let's go and pick him up. Are the boys OK here with you?" Becks asked Jason.

"Yeah, of course they are. Who wants to drive the tractor?" Jacob bellowed loudly, as he scooped up the boys and swiftly whisked them away from the kitchen in his powerful embrace.

Becks anxiously chauffeured Joan to the hospital. A cloud of nervousness overcame them. After a lengthy discharge process, Bob was finally released. Seated in a wheelchair, Becks guided him towards the hospital's entrance. As the doors swung open, a gust of fresh air greeted Bob, reminiscent of a blissful spring day. He tilted his head up, shut his eyes, and savoured every sensation of the invigorating breeze.

"Mum, why don't you wait here with Dad. I'll go and get the car, he looks like he's enjoying sitting there," Becks said, smiling.

She walked to the car and her phone rang, it was Connor.

"Hi, are you OK?" she asked giddily.

"Yes, you sound happy," Connor replied.

"I am, I really am. I forgot how beautiful this place can be. I'm at the hospital with Mum. Dad's just been discharged. Do you mind if I call you back?" Becks asked.

"Yes, of course. I'll be on the 5:02 pm train, so I should be with you for about half six. Are you still ok to pick me up?" Connor asked.

"Yes, of course I am, I can't wait to see you. I've missed you," Becks replied.

"Me too, I'm looking forward to having you all home, the house is far too quiet without you," he said.

"It must be, see you tonight, love you," she replied, lovingly.

She pulled her car up to the front doors of the hospital, helped Bob into the front seat, reached over him to fetch his seat belt, and buckled him in as if he were a child. Bob lifted his arms and smiled at his daughter. She was there, helping him, and her presence brought him immense happiness.

"Is that OK, Dad?" Becks asked.

"Perfect, just perfect," he replied. She started the ten-mile journey back to the farmhouse.

"Right, I'm only going to tell you this once, you are to rest, Dad. I mean it. Jason and Jacob have got the farm covered, with a little help from Logan and Rory, and you need to let us look after you, OK?" Becks said sternly. Without uttering a single word, Bob gently rested his hand on Becks', giving it a reassuring pat. A warm smile graced his face as he gazed out of the window, admiring the green fields. He was lost in his thoughts, thrilled to be breathing and enjoying his family by his side.

Upon arriving home, Bob was greeted by everyone, who gathered around him. The boys assisted him out of the car and positioned his beloved chair in front of the TV, along with the footstool placed conveniently in front of him.

"Cup of tea, old man?" Jacob asked, his hand resting lovingly on his father's shoulder.

"Yes, and a biscuit," Bob replied slowly, in his deep voice. The entire family gathered in the living room, feeling thankful and united after being apart for so long.

As they caught up with each other, Jason eagerly shared the latest news about the farm, putting Bob's worries to rest. The room was soon filled with laughter as Rory and Logan entertained everyone with their hilarious stories. With hearts full of affection, Bob and Joan gazed upon their grandsons, love radiating from their eyes.

Becks then announced, "So, Dad, Jason has something to ask you,"

"Oh, what's that?" Bob asked, as he cleared his throat. Jason took the ring box from the old wooden side dresser, and walked towards Bob.

"I want to ask Julie to marry me. Mum found Grandma's ring last night, and Becks took it to be cleaned. Is it OK with you if I give it to her?" Jason asked.,

Bob looked at his eldest son with such pride, "When did this all bloody happen? Yes, of course it is, Son, come here," Bob said, as he flung his arms around his boy.

"It was Becks, she asked and, I don't know, it seems right. So, I'm thinking of doing it tonight, after dinner. What do you think?" Jason asked.

"Can you wait until Connor arrives? He's getting in at 6:30 pm, How about I get fish and chips on the way back for us all, then you can pop the question after her mushy peas?" Becks excitedly suggested.

"Oh, yeah, a chippy tea, thanks Becks. Wow, I'm going to do this," Jason said, a nervous chuckle escaping from his lips.

With the boys in tow, Becks headed towards the train station, and the sheer happiness on Connor's face upon their arrival was undeniable.

"Hey, I've missed you guys," Connor said, as he hugged them tightly.

"We missed you, Daddy. Guess what? I drove the tractor," Logan said.

"You did? Way to go buddy, well done," Connor replied. Hand in hand, the four of them strolled along, making their way towards the car.

Their destination was set, a delightful fish and chips joint to pick up the pre-engagement dinner. However, before returning home with their savoury treat, Becks couldn't contain her excitement any longer. With a mix of anticipation and thrill, she revealed the plans for the evening, her enthusiasm radiating dangerously.

"So, after dinner, Jason is going to propose to Julie, I can't believe it, it's so exciting. Honestly, I'm made up for him. You should have seen Dad's face when he asked about the ring," Becks exclaimed with a grin, brimming with excitement, she spoke rapidly.

"It all sounds very exciting," Connor expressed with an element of disappointment.

As she made a quick stop at the off-licence, she picked up three bottles of Prosecco and a few beers. A wide smile adorned her face, and Connor could see a noticeable transformation in her demeanour, she seemed calm and content. It had been a while since he noticed that spark in her eyes, their daily routine back in their hometown was constantly set at a rapid pace, leaving no room for relaxation.

While she drove them back home, they engaged in lively conversation, and the boys were exploding with happiness. Surprisingly, all of this unfolded without any involvement from Connor, which concerned him.

"Dad's home, too. He still needs a lot of rest, but he's doing well. I'm just so grateful the surgery worked," Becks said.

"That is good news," Connor replied. "

"I thought he was going to cry when Jason asked about the ring," Becks continued.

"You seem happy, different almost," Connor added.

"Different how?" Becks asked.

"I don't know, I haven't seen you this happy in a very long time," Connor replied.

"I am happy. It's been very stressful, but it's also been a wonderful week, being here with my family, Connor. I've felt at home, for the first time in years," she replied. Despite his lingering anxiety and guilt, he was determined to bring joy to his wife. A feeling of being left behind overwhelmed him, as he believed he could no longer fulfil his wife's happiness.

Upon arriving at the house, the boys dashed inside, while Connor retrieved his case from the boot and Becks carried the fish and chips along with the alcohol.

"We're home," Becks shouted. Connor's face showed a surprised look upon hearing these words coming from Becks' mouth. This wasn't her home. Regrettably, he could sense the distance in his wife's demeanour, after just a few days of being apart.

"In the kitchen," Jason shouted back. Connor entered his in-laws' home once more, feeling uneasy, but determined to make an effort and fit in. He placed his belongings in the bedroom before heading downstairs to the kitchen. The table had been prepared, with food already served, and everyone was enjoying their meal at rapid speed directly from the paper wrapping. However, Connor carefully transferred his fish and chips onto a plate before slowly savouring each bite. His face twisted in revulsion as he witnessed the appalling table etiquette of his wife's family. Everyone was engaged in conversation, discussing topics like horses, sheep, cows, and tractors, subjects that didn't interest Connor. Even Becks was participating, further emphasising his sense of being an outsider in the group.

In the cosy lounge, they gathered after dinner, enjoying the warmth of the roaring log fire while watching TV. Suddenly,

Jason grabbed everyone's attention by lowering the volume, causing all eyes to fixate on him.

"What are you doing? I was watching that," Julie asked, with a startled look on her face.

"Jules, I have something for you, and something to ask you. We've been together for a while now, and I was wondering if you would like to be my wife?" Jason said, as he pulled the ring box out of his jeans pocket and opened it.

"Jason! Where has this come from? Oh, my goodness, yes, yes, I would love to be your wife," Julie answered, as she flung her arms around him. They kissed and looked over at the rest of the family, receiving smiles from all around.

"Did you all know about this?" Julie asked naively.

"We may have known a little something," Becks stated, smiling.

"Congratulations," Joan said, as she stood up, walked towards them and hugged them both.

"Now, that there ring was my mother's ring. My father gave that to my mother on her twenty-first birthday. They were married for over sixty years, and I hope it brings you the same," Bob said in a deep voice, his Northern accent prominent, as he sat with his arms over his stomach and his legs upright resting on the footstool.

"Bob, thank you, it's beautiful, I will cherish it. Thank you, everyone," Julie said, as she looked down and admired the ring on her finger.

The room was brimming with joy and warm embraces, creating an atmosphere of pure happiness. It was a truly delightful moment, and Becks felt immense pride to be a part of it. Becks strolled into the kitchen with a grin on her face, retrieving nine mugs from the cupboard, along with a bottle of Prosecco and a bottle of milk from the fridge. Connor entered the room behind her, curious about what she was up to.

"Do you need any help?" he asked.

"Yes, please, can you bring the mugs in?" Becks asked.

"Mugs? Have they not got any champagne flutes?" Connor asked distastefully.

"No, Connor! They haven't got any champagne flutes!" Becks said sternly, as she brushed past him in anger. He immediately sensed his wife's annoyance. He gathered the handles of the mugs in his hand and quietly followed her.

"Let's toast the happy couple," Becks said, as she waved the Prosecco in the air and smiled. Jason popped the cork and bubbles were added to six of the non-matching mugs that had been collected over the years.

"Milk for you, boys, and you, Dad," Becks said, as she handed drinks to her family.

"I just want to say a few words before we toast this engagement. This last week has been tricky, for all of us, but seeing you all come together, work hard and keep everything going here, well it means a lot to me and your mother. Rebecca, it's been very nice seeing you every day, and you being here for your mum like that. Well, thank you, I know it can't have been easy for you to be away from your home. So, to the next exciting chapter. It's been a while since we had a good Pritchard wedding, to Jason and Julie," Bob said, as he coughed. Becks' smile masked the unease she felt, she knew there was an element of sarcasm about her wedding in that little speech.

"To Jason and Julie," Becks said quietly, as they all raised their cups in the air. Connor grimaced as he took a sip of Prosecco from his tea-stained mug.

Afterwards, they spent an hour chatting about wedding plans and admiring Jason's romantic proposal. Julie was nestled between Jason's legs, leaning against some cushions on the floor with his arms around her. His cosy grey socks, with several holes, revealed his big toe peeking out.

"I was extremely nervous when I proposed, I had this entire evening planned. We had dinner at The Shard, a client of mine had booked us the best table with a view overlooking London, and I paid the pianist to play her favourite song, it was magical, wasn't it love?" Connor so smugly said.

"Yes, it was, it was beautiful," Becks nodded in agreement, lowering her head in embarrassment, while everyone's gaze fixated on Connor.

The impressive displays and boastful behaviour did not dazzle them. Becks came to the realisation that a deeper purpose in life existed, one that extended far beyond the superficiality of extravagance and using money as a means to find happiness.

"Well, I wanted everyone here to share our moment, so I hope it was special enough?" Jason asked Julie, as he looked at her lovingly, and brushed her hair behind her ear.

"It was perfect and so unexpected, how did this even come about?" Julie asked.

"It was Becks, she made me see what I've got with you, and I need to lock you down," Jason said, as he looked into Julie's eyes and smiled.

"So, it's just Jacob left now. When are you going to find yourself a nice lady friend?" Becks said, as she kicked Jacob on the leg. A heavy silence fell upon the room, causing everyone's expressions to turn sombre as their eyes fixated on Becks. Jacob, showing signs of embarrassment and being ashamed, averted his gaze downwards.

"What have I said?" Becks asked.

"Nothing, love, nothing," Joan replied.

"Right, I think I'm ready for bed," Bob said suddenly, as he went to stand up.

"Here, Dad, I'll help you," Jacob said, as he stood up briskly. Jacob lent a helping hand to Bob, guiding him through the hallway and up the stairs.

"What was that?" Becks asked Jason and Joan quietly. They looked at each other.

"Jacob is gay," Jason added.

"He's what? Since when?" Becks asked, in disbelief.

"He told us about a year ago, then told Dad about nine months ago. It didn't go down well with Dad," Jason added, as Joan kept quiet.

"Why didn't you tell me?" Becks asked.

"Well, we don't see you, it wasn't something we wanted to say over the phone, and Jacob wants to keep it quiet," Joan added.

"Well, thanks for keeping that from me, I feel like a right idiot now," Becks said. She harboured a hidden frustration and experienced a sense of alienation within the confines of her own family.

Overwhelmed by irritation and a sense of detachment, she opted to depart from the living room quietly. Becks went upstairs to find the boys playing cards on the bed,

"OK, you two, bath and bed, it's very late!" Becks said, as she dived on the bed in between them and tickled them playfully. With a desire to redirect her thoughts and find pleasure in the company of her little ones, she sought ways to entertain and bond with them. In this serene environment, Becks experienced a profound sense of relaxation. It made her feel like a nurturing mother, as she was able to dedicate quality time and undivided attention to her children. The positive behaviour they exhibited further reinforced her contentment. The boys ran to the bathroom and jumped into the bathtub filled with bubbles. Connor discreetly trailed behind Becks, and, quietly approaching her from the back, he pulled her close, surrounding her with his embrace.

"I feel like I haven't had two minutes with you, come here Mrs Jones," he whispered, as he lay a gentle kiss on her cheek.

"I know, we'll be back home soon, then it will be back to normal," Becks said, as she turned towards him, kissed his lips abruptly and walked to the bathroom. After tucking the boys into bed, Becks left Connor upstairs and made her way back downstairs to join her family for an important conversation.

As she entered the living room, she discovered her mother and two brothers still seated in front of the TV in silence.

"Jacob, I'm sorry, I had no idea," Becks said in front of them all. Jacob sat alone in the armchair, with Jason and Julie cuddled up on the sofa, and Joan stood at the kitchen door with a cloth in her hand.

"You didn't know, it's OK, we just don't talk about it, especially in front of Dad," Jacob replied.

"Yes, I get it, but why didn't you tell me?" Becks asked.

"We rarely speak. What was I meant to do, ring you up and say, 'hey, sis, we haven't spoken in six months, by the way, I'm gay?' Doesn't work like that," Jacob said.

"I'm sorry, I guess I've been really out of the loop," Becks replied.

"Well, you're here now, that's what counts," Joan added, as she placed her hand on Becks' upper arm. Becks gazed at her younger brothers, who had matured into adults and she hadn't been there to witness it.

Feeling a sense of detachment from her own family, she stood in silence for a few minutes as Jason, Jacob and Julie continued to watch television.

"I'm off to bed. Goodnight, guys, and congratulations you two," Jacob said, standing up and walking out of the living room. Becks stood in utter discomfort as Jacob walked past her.

"Listen, you didn't know, don't stress about it," Jason said, trying to comfort his sister.

"So, what did Dad do, when he told him?" Becks asked quietly, as she moved into the lounge and sat on the floor.

"It all kicked off, he threw Jacob out and told him not to come back, told him he wasn't welcome in the house and he didn't want him on the farm. Jacob left for a few weeks and went to stay at his friend's house. Then, he came home after about three weeks and told Dad that he would try and that he'd broken it off with his partner. He also said he wasn't going to have another one either," Jason continued.

"So he had a boyfriend, then broke up with him?" Becks asked.

"Yeah, this guy he was living with, he wanted to be out there with the relationship and Jacob said no, so it ended," Jason replied.

"It's so sad – he has to stop being who he is to live here?" Becks asked.

"It's not like that. It's just Dad won't tolerate him being openly gay and Jacob is OK with that. He told Dad that he wouldn't and that's it, Dad said he could come home," Jason said casually.

"That's ridiculous, he can't control him, so what if he's gay," Becks said loudly.

"Keep your voice down, Rebecca," Joan said soberly.

"And are you OK with this, Mum?" Becks asked.

"Jacob is home, where he belongs, that's all that matters," Joan replied.

"So, his happiness doesn't matter?" Becks asked.

"He will be happy. He is happy, he has his family around him," Joan replied.

"I'm speechless," Becks said.

In utter disbelief, she gazed at the scene before her and swiftly made her way out of the living room, heading towards the stairs. She walked to her room,

"You'll never believe this, so, he isn't allowed to be gay. I mean, what year are we living in? Poor Jacob, he's forced to live a life where he can't be happy to appease my father!" Becks said in a semi-silenced, yet semi-raised, voice to Connor, who was lying on the bed.

"Becks, be quiet, the walls are thin, remember," Connor replied.

"I don't care. This week, everyone has been so happy, it's been relaxed, and all because he hasn't been here. I don't know how they live like this," Becks said, as she paced up and down.

"Don't get involved in this, please. You'll wind yourself up and then it will all explode, it always does. Just leave it," Connor replied.

"Fine. It's just wrong," Becks said.

"Wrong that they didn't tell you?" Connor asked.

"Yes, I guess so. I'm an outsider, Connor, and I don't want to be," Becks replied angrily.

As they settled into bed, the boys were asleep on the mattresses laid out on the floor. Connor and Becks snuggled up together, with Becks resting her head on his shoulder while he gently caressed her back.

"I've missed you and I'm sorry for everything, my behaviour has been appalling. I've had a stern word with myself and I'm truly sorry, it will never happen again," he whispered.

"It's OK, just talk to me. We both have stressful jobs, Connor, and I understand it's hard to juggle everything, but we mustn't push each other away. I've already lost this side of my family, I don't want to lose us, too," she replied.

"I don't either," he whispered. With a gentle kiss, he then moved to lay himself on top of her. Slowly, he undressed her, removing her nightdress and sliding her knickers down.

As their passion intensified, he lowered his pyjama bottoms and they became one, with Connor lying on top of her.

"We shouldn't be doing this here," Becks said, as she took a deep sigh. Becks was feeling disconnected, but she didn't want to deprive her husband of his much-needed relief. She yielded to his persuasion and wrapped her arms around him.

"Why not? I've missed you, I've missed this," he said, as he thrust inside her, trying hard to feel that connection again. He longed for Suzy to be out of his mind, he needed to focus on Becks.

As he gazed at her, Suzy's image suddenly appeared, causing him to rest his head on her shoulder. With closed eyes, he surrendered himself to the moment, wanting nothing more than to cherish his wife's presence. They lay together after their quiet and calm sex before Becks put her night clothes back on and walked down the hall to the bathroom. Connor slipped on his pants and dabbed himself with a tissue before glancing at his two sons peacefully sleeping.

After freshening up, Becks switched off the bathroom light and quietly shut the door, only to hear the unmistakable sounds of the soon-to-be newlyweds next door sealing their vows. Standing outside Jacob's bedroom, she could hear the television on, and felt a wave of sadness for him being alone. She hesitated to knock, raising her hand towards the door before stopping herself. With a heavy heart, she lowered her head and retreated to her old bedroom. As she crawled back into bed, she planted a gentle kiss on Connor's cheek before rolling over and drifting off to sleep. Meanwhile, Connor found himself unable to divert his attention from the ceiling above. His restless fingers moved continuously, his mind longing to banish thoughts of this woman. But how could he possibly achieve that?

They savoured their final day together, walking Bob slowly around the farm, while Becks prepared a delicious chicken roast dinner for lunch. She wanted to share one last meal with them, uncertain when they would all be together again. Becks chose to heed Connor's suggestion and stay silent regarding Jacob, noticing the strained relationship between him and her father but opting to stay out of it, no matter her own emotions.

On Saturday afternoon, after their family lunch, Jacob was in the cow shed while the rest of the family stayed indoors. Becks decided to take a stroll, fully aware that she would come across him.

"Do you need some help?" Becks asked, as she stood in her wellies.

"No, just fed the last of them," Jacob said.

"How many have you got?" Becks asked,

"374!" Jacob replied.

"Wow, that sounds like a lot of work," Becks replied.

"It's a lot of money, and that's what we're doing here, making money," Jacob replied, as he continued to work, ensuring not to make eye contact with Becks.

"Jacob, I'm sorry," Becks said.

"About what?" Jacob asked.

"You, and Dad, and your life, I mean, what are you going to do?" Becks asked.

"Nothing. I'll just live life like this until, well, something happens to him," Jacob replied.

"That's intense, so you'll abide by his rules, like a child. He could be around for years, Jacob," Becks said.

"Becks, what do you want from me? I have nothing else – I have no skills. I can't just walk away like you did," Jacob replied.

"You can do whatever you want to do. You're a thirty-two-year-old man, living in his mother and father's house, not being able to be true to yourself because Dad doesn't approve," Becks added.

"You don't get it, I need them. I don't know anything else," Jacob replied.

"That makes me sad. You should be allowed to live life the way you choose," Becks replied.

"I don't know what else to do. My relationship ended because I couldn't commit and so I had no choice but to come home, I've numbed myself to the feeling," Jacob answered, as he battled with his emotions.

"Come here," Becks said, walking up to her baby brother and hugging him tightly.

"I'm fine," Jacob hesitantly replied, as he walked towards his sister.

"I do know how you feel, it's like being in a trap living here. If you ever need to escape, you call me and come to me, I'll help you," Becks said, as she held him tight.

"I'm fine, I am. And I will be happy, I have to be," Jacob said, as he rubbed his nose with the back of his hand and carried on with his work. Becks gazed at her brother, his heart shattered, yet she felt powerless to rescue him.

After enjoying breakfast on Sunday, they bid goodbye and headed home together. The boys felt a tinge of sadness as they left the farm, while Becks was anxious about parting ways, yet secretly looking forward to sleeping in her bed and returning to her routine. Upon arriving home at 1 pm, the boys dashed upstairs to indulge in playing with the toys they had deeply missed.

"It smells very fresh in here," Becks said.

"Does it?" Connor asked.

"Yes, it does, have you cleaned up, Mr Jones?" Becks asked, smiling.

"I might have, I wanted you to come home to a fresh, clean house," he said, as he cuddled and kissed her neck.

"You've even plumped the cushions, you never plump the cushions," she expressed, smiling.

"Well, maybe things change. I love you, and I want us to be happy, a new start, right here," he said as he stood in front of her, held her hands up by her head and kissed her lips tenderly.

"OK, the online shopping is showing arrival at two, can we have a takeaway tonight?" Becks asked.

"Of course, Chinese?" Connor replied.

"Ooh, yes please," Becks replied. She was happy to be home.

After putting away the groceries and completing three loads of washing, it was finally bedtime. She settled into her cosy, soft and spacious bed that offered a blissful escape from uncomfortable mattress springs. With a pile of emails awaiting her attention, she couldn't help but feel a sense of reluctance about returning to work the next day. Logging into her online banking, she discovered that Kerry had once again failed to pay her rent on 1 March, leaving her feeling frustrated and anxious once more.

The following day, it felt as though she'd never left. The familiar routine resumed and they were once again living life in the fast lane. As she arrived at school, her colleagues and friends expressed their concern and, after bidding farewell to her boys, she settled down at her desk. Without wasting a moment, she immediately reached out to Kerry. She began to type, saying each word out loud.

'Hi Kerry, I hope you're well. The rent has not cleared again this month. I appreciate it's now the 4th, I waited until this morning with it being the weekend. Could you kindly look into this please?' She read it aloud again to herself and pressed send. An hour went by without a response, causing her stomach to churn with worry. She carried on with her day, checking her online banking as usual, but there was no indication of the rent payment.

By 4 pm, there was still no reply, so she decided to call the estate agent to inform them of the situation.

"Mrs Jones, we're so sorry, we didn't hear back from you so we didn't complete the checks as we thought you were sorted," the estate agent said.

"What? What do you mean you didn't complete the checks? I didn't hear from you so I took it everything was fine," Becks replied.

"I'm sorry, there seems to have been some miscommunication, we'll write to her now and feedback once we get in touch with her," the estate agent replied.

"I just want you to take over the management. My father is unwell and I just don't have time for this every month. Can you please write to her to tell her that you're now managing the tenancy?" Becks asked.

"Yes, certainly, I'll get onto this today," the estate agent replied.

"What do I do if she doesn't pay?" Becks asked.

"Well, we'll contact her, but you have to wait until she misses two full payments before we can take any action," the estate agent replied.

"What do you mean? So, if she doesn't answer your letter this month, I have to wait until April?" Becks asked.

"Yes. If she doesn't reply this month, and doesn't pay on 1 April, we then have to apply to the court for her to be evicted, which can take six to eight weeks," the estate agent said.

"Another six weeks after that?" Becks exclaimed in a raised voice down the phone.

"Yes, I'm afraid so," the estate agent confirmed.

"That's ludicrous. So, she gets to live there for three, possibly four months, rent-free, and there's nothing I can do about it?" Becks asked.

"Yes, but once the eviction notice has been given by the court, she'll have one month to vacate," the estate agent said.

"For God's sake, what kind of stupid law is that?" Becks asked. The phone went silent.

"We'll get a letter out to her today, Mrs Jones," the estate agent repeated.

"Right, just manage this on my behalf from now on and, please, keep me in the loop," Becks stated, and put the phone down. Stress and anxiety churned in her stomach and disbelief washed over her, as she grappled with the audacity of someone being so rude and disrespectful.

On her way home, Becks decided to take a detour and pass by the old house. To her surprise, Kerry's car was parked on the driveway. Feeling a mix of boldness and annoyance, she parked her car on the side of the road, stepped out, and confidently walked up to the front door. She pressed the doorbell and patiently waited for a response, but after a minute of silence, she decided to give it another try. With no response for a second time, she strolled towards the small front lawn and glanced through the downstairs window. The house appeared neat, with all their belongings in place, except for an unsightly glass table supported by two gaudy gold spikes at the centre of the living room. With a disgusted expression, Becks scrunched up her face in distaste.

Kerry was nowhere to be seen through the window, prompting Becks to return to her car. As she glanced at the upstairs windows one final time, she noticed the master bedroom curtains twitching. Intrigued, she paused for a moment and gazed up at the window with a sense of curiosity, but then everything went still, so she opened the driver-side door and got into her car.

"Mummy, who lives there now?" Logan asked.

"Another family sweetheart," Becks replied.

"So why are we back here if someone else lives there?" Logan continued.

"Because Daddy and Mummy still own the house, someone else is paying us to live there. Well, they're meant to be!" Becks replied, muttering under her breath. Kerry glanced out from the upstairs window as she watched Becks drive away.

Becks was feeling a mix of anger and disappointment as she drove home. Despite cooking dinner and feeding the boys, her mind was preoccupied. The conversation with the estate agent and the stories Kerry had told her left her feeling annoyed with herself.

When Connor got back to the house, she poured her heart out over dinner, sharing every detail until tears started to flow down her cheeks.

"I feel so stupid!" she said as she placed her hands over her eyes.

"It's OK, let the estate agent do their job and we'll sort it," he replied.

"What if she refuses to pay? Then we have to take her to court. We can't afford this. It's all my fault, why did I rush into this? I should have waited until after New Year. She was so convincing. Do you think this was her plan all along?" Becks asked.

"It's one payment but, yes, it's possible, you can never tell with these people, Becks. The estate agent is also at fault, you asked them to do the checks and they didn't," Connor replied, in an attempt to comfort his wife.

"Yes, but I gave her the bloody keys!" she shouted.

"There's nothing we can do now; we just need to ride this out. It's one to two months, Becks and we'll either have our house back, or we'll have the money. Try to be calm," Connor said tenderly.

"I had a look through the window. The place looked tidy and all our furniture was still in the same place, the only thing it looks like she has brought herself is this God-awful glass table. The glass is on two gold spikes, it looked like something out of a junk shop," Becks said in disgust.

Throughout the night, sleep eluded her as she continuously checked her bank accounts and messages. Kerry had read her message but was ignoring her deliberately, which only fuelled Becks' growing frustration. Overwhelmed with worry, she went to the office and meticulously combed through the contract, desperately searching for any loophole that could work in her favour. Unfortunately, the contract held no power, leaving her with no option but to abide by the law that favoured tenants over the rightful owner of the house. Connor appeared in the doorway.

"What are you doing?" he asked.

"I have no idea. I'm just trying to find something – a loophole – to get her out," Becks said in desperation, as she gathered the paperwork together and put it back in the file.

"If it goes to court, she probably won't even show up, Becks. She'd have to be pretty bold. She might even be out before it comes to that. Come on, come back to bed, try to rest," Connor said, holding out his hand.

Becks carefully returned the file to its place in the cupboard, before intertwining her fingers with her husband's. As they lay side by side in bed, their eyes locked in a tender gaze and a sense of deep connection overcame them.

"Thank you," Becks said.

"For what?" Connor asked.

"For being you. You're a good man, you could have gone mad at me for this, but you're always so understanding," Becks replied.

"Come on now, we'll get through this, everything will be fine," Connor replied, as he kissed her on the nose and held her tenderly.

March came to an end and Kerry still hadn't responded to Becks. When the estate agent had called her, Kerry denied them as her landlord and abruptly ended the call. By 1 April, no rent had been paid, prompting Becks to reach out to the estate agent to inquire about the next steps.

"So, the next step is to contact a solicitor and apply to court?" Becks asked.

"Yes, they'll guide you on the process and put in a request for an eviction notice. We'll also serve her with an eviction notice and explain that you've initiated legal action," the estate agent confirmed.

"What would happen if I went to the house and confronted her?" Becks asked.

"She could have you done for harassment. If she calls the police it could be you facing charges," the estate agent explained.

"She's in my house!" Becks exclaimed.

The audacity of this woman left her in disbelief, questioning every word Kerry had spoken. Despite attempts to reach out, there was still no response by the end of April, and with the property appearing to be occupied, it was off-limits to Becks and the estate agent. The court had scheduled the hearing for Monday, 20 May at 10 am. It was a seemingly fast turnaround, yet it felt like an eternity for Becks and Connor, who were now three months behind on rent and buried under legal expenses.

As Sunday, 19 May approached, the evening before the court date, Becks carefully laid out her clothes for the next day.

"You will attend court with me in the morning, won't you?" Becks asked.

"Of course I will. We'll drop the boys off, leave your car at school, go to court, and then I'll drop you back at school. Stop worrying, we'll get this sorted," Connor replied.

"Just how bloody wrong is this? This nasty, vindictive woman, lying to me, ignoring me. I feel ridiculously stupid to have fallen for her lies," Becks said.

"You're not stupid, you're trusting, and a nice person, there's a huge difference. People who do this are wrong, they think they are better than everyone. If she was struggling, she could have contacted you. We're understanding people, Becks, and we would've helped her. It's the fact she's blatantly ignoring you that's so annoying," Connor rambled at a fast pace, his anger evident.

"I'm speechless, I'm furious with her," Becks replied.

"People like this think they can go through life living and sponging off hard-working people, it's disgusting. And don't even get me started on the law, what a bloody joke. If I didn't pay my mortgage for three months, they'd be in here repossessing our house. It's laughable that these tenants have so many damn rights. I've a mind to go round there tonight and bang the damn door down!" Connor expressed passionately.

"The last thing we need is you getting arrested. She's not worth it. She's a thief and a liar," Becks said, as she stood shaking.

"It'll be OK. Tomorrow we'll have an eviction date, and then she has to move out," he said, as he came close to Becks and held her.

"Thank you. I'm so sorry I caused all of this," Becks said, resting her head on his chest. Becks had always been familiar with stress. However, in all the chaos of her busy life, she'd never experienced anything quite like this. It was consuming her, devouring her from within.

Becks tossed and turned all night, her lack of sleep leading to a wave of anxiety she'd never experienced before. Watching the hours tick by only made her more nervous, as she prepared to face the courtroom for the first time in her life.

The following morning, they arrived at school in separate cars. Becks dropped the boys off to the staff at breakfast club, and they drove to court in Connor's vehicle.

After parking, Connor displayed the pay and display ticket on the windscreen before they strolled hand in hand across the car park, exuding the image of a polished, professional couple. The solicitor and estate agent welcomed them upon arrival.

"Good morning. If she doesn't show up this morning, it's a good thing because it means the eviction notice can be given today. Which means within a month you'll have your keys back. If she doesn't vacate by the specified date, then the bailiffs will go in and remove her," the solicitor said. Becks anxiously nodded, her lips parched and her leg tapping restlessly. They waited patiently, Connor attempting to hide his anxiety and provide comfort to Becks.

Eventually, they were summoned to Court Room Three and they entered through the imposing wooden doors, taking their seats as the solicitor removed his paperwork from his file. Becks sat upright, maintaining a confident posture with her head held high and legs crossed, meticulously smoothing out her skirt, blouse, and jacket.

Suddenly, the doors swung open and in walked Kerry, exuding boldness and confidence.
"That's her, the cheek!" Becks said, as she squeezed Connor's hand. Kerry glanced over at Becks before locking eyes with Connor and flashing a flirtatious smile. Connor's face dropped, his blood ran cold, and he had a sense of impending doom as he saw her face. His heart began to race and his palms became sweaty. From the soles of his feet to the crown of his head, a fiery sensation coursed through him, igniting every inch of his being with a scorching warmth. A face he should not have recognised but, unfortunately, he did. Stood there in the flesh, it was Suzy. His guilty secret was his tenant!

He swallowed hard and stared at her, a feeling of nausea waved inside of him.
"She's smiling at me, how dare she!" Becks whispered.
"What's her name?" Connor whispered back, without moving an inch.
"Kerry Reed," Becks replied. Connor felt sick. His throat felt as if it was about to close. he began to breathe fast, and he fidgeted with his tie, trying to loosen it.
"What's wrong?" Becks asked, as she placed her hand on his leg, which was jittering erratically.

"All rise," came from the court.

The judge made his entrance and the battle commenced. Becks' and Connor's lawyer presented his case, followed by Kerry's lawyer who took the floor. And let me tell you, she was impressive. She recounted Kerry's recent escape from a terrible marriage, an abusive relationship that had left her financially embarrassed. She expressed regret for not reaching out to the landlord and apologised sincerely, feeling a deep sense of shame. With the confirmation of a new relationship, she decided to have her partner move in and contribute financially. Kerry's attorney assured the court that May's rent would be fully covered by Friday, with a payment arrangement for the outstanding balance.

Becks, feeling helpless, sat anxiously, her bottom lip caught between her teeth. She longed to rise and protest, but Kerry emerged victorious as the judge granted her until Friday to settle the rent in its entirety, warning of eviction if she failed to do so. Kerry's solicitor had devised a payment plan that the judge ultimately approved. The plan allowed Kerry to settle the two months' worth of outstanding payments over the next three months. Becks and Connor were taken aback by the decision. However, the outcome was final, and unfortunately they were defeated. Rising to their feet, they made their way to the door. Connor, feeling uneasy, stood behind Becks, making himself look small and lacking in power.

As he glanced over at Suzy, she smiled and winked at him, causing him to quickly divert his gaze and wrap his arm around his wife's back. Annoyed and frustrated, they left the courtroom, with Connor feeling petrified.
"What the hell happened?" Becks asked their solicitor.
"She has until Friday. Chances are, she won't pay, then we can serve the notice. If she does pay then at least you have your money. Let the estate agents handle this and we can look at the small print and ask her to leave. The best thing is not to get into any arguments with her, stick to the law and the facts and you'll soon have your house back. I know it's not easy but try not to worry, it will be sorted, one way or another," the lawyer replied.

Becks and Connor walked outside together, their hands intertwined, but Kerry was nowhere to be seen near the courthouse. Connor gallantly opened the car door for Becks and made his way to the driver's seat as Kerry zoomed past them in her flashy Mercedes, wearing a self-satisfied grin and oversized sunglasses. Connor froze in astonishment, his mouth agape, as Kerry sped away down the road.

Driving back to school Connor was in a daze and Becks was furious.

"How the hell has she got away with this? A new boyfriend? She's like a hooker, I can just imagine the type of man she has funding this ridiculous lifestyle." Becks continued to talk incessantly, while Connor remained silent, completely stunned and clueless about how to deal with the situation at hand.

"I don't know," Connor said quietly

"Why are you so quiet?" Becks asked.

"I'm just processing it. We'll sort this, try not to worry. We'll sort this out," Connor said, determined to get to the bottom of this mess. After leaving Becks at the school gates, he quickly kissed her goodbye and sped off. As Becks entered the school, her worried colleagues gathered around her, but she wasn't feeling up to being a head teacher that day. Making her way to her office, she tossed her bag onto her desk and let out a frustrated sigh. Sitting down, she covered her face with her hands, feeling her cheeks flush with anger. Taking a deep breath, she regained her composure, switched on her computer, and got down to work.

Connor, now alone, loosened his tie fully and unbuttoned his top button, his breathing quickened and his heart raced with intensity.

"Fuck! Fuck!" he shouted to himself, hitting his steering wheel. Without hesitation, he steered his car towards the old house, parking just behind the familiar Mercedes. Exiting his vehicle, he slammed the door shut and briskly made his way to the front entrance. Despite the temptation to unlock the door with his key, he resisted and instead pressed the doorbell. As he waited, he stood with his right hand on his hip, absentmindedly rubbing his mouth with his left hand.

As she answered the door, she smiled and said, "Well, hello there, you, I wondered how long it would take you."

"What the actual fuck do you think you're doing? Who even are you?" Connor exclaimed. He forcefully entered the house and firmly closed the door behind them.

"Down boy!" Suzy said, laughing.

"Don't you laugh at me, don't you dare fucking laugh at me, what the hell do you think you're doing?" he asked.

"What? Did you not check any of the documents that your stupid wife brought home?" she asked.

"Don't call her stupid, how dare you!" Connor said, as he erupted in fury, his voice booming with emotion.

"Right, OK, let's just cool this. We can go over the small print but, the thing is, we are where we are. So, here's what I need, I need you to transfer two thousand pounds to me every month to make sure this rent is paid and I can meet the payment plan. If you don't, then I'll tell your precious little Becks everything," Suzy confidently explained.

"Are you for real? Now you're blackmailing me?" Connor said, smirking angrily.

"You are a clever boy," Suzy replied sarcastically.

"Why are you doing this? Do you know what? Go ahead, tell her, she won't believe you, look at the fucking state of you. What was I thinking going anywhere near you?" he said with disgust and disappointment.

"She won't believe me? Well, let's see shall we," Suzy said, as she got her phone out of the back pocket of her jeans, typed in the code and proceeded to reveal a collection of snapshots capturing him asleep and unclothed within the confines of her hotel room. Alongside these images, she proudly displayed his discarded garments strewn across the floor, a snapshot of his driver's licence, and a glimpse of his wallet. He felt lightheaded, his heart pounding in his ribcage.

"You took pictures of me? Why, Suzy? Why? Was this all just a trick? Did you know who I was all this time?" Connor asked.

"What do you think? Do you honestly think I would be interested in you? This isn't hard to do, in fact, it's quite easy. Your wife promoted the house on social media, I clicked on her profile and I noticed your profile too, which I must say is terribly boring. But you seemed alright, naive, average looking," she expressed, raising her eyebrows.

"I can't believe you," Connor said.

"I then spotted the logo on your gym t-shirt and I thought, Bingo! That's my way in, so I joined. God, you were so easy, desperate if I'm honest, and I could see how bored you were. I mean, come on, does she ever even get on top? How vanilla your life must be being married to her!" Kerry said confidently.

"Don't you fucking—" Connor interrupted.

But before he could finish his sentence, Kerry continued "You wanted me. You were dying to have some fun, some passion, and yeah, I used you. To be honest, I was pleasantly surprised, I thought you would be useless in bed, but you're quite good, hence my last visit to your house. I already had my evidence, so that was just a bonus. I could see from the first time I saw you that you wanted me, she would never allow you to do what you did to me. Oh, and getting you to the hotel so I could get your picture, my God, you caved so quickly, 'I came here to tell you to stop,'" she mimicked. "Like shit, you wanted me. I knew you hadn't seen my ID by your reaction at the gym – you clearly didn't recognise me. You're so naïve, Connor, stupid almost, quite laughable," Suzy said, chuckling.

He clenched his teeth together; he had no idea what his next move entailed.

"I'm not fucking around, now you listen to me, you crazy little bitch, I want you out of this house by the end of the week, do you understand me?" Connor replied, as he stepped closer, his face inches away from hers.

"Come on big man, show me what you've got." Suzy stood on her tiptoes to meet him face-to-face.

"You're a con artist, what even is this? You make a life out of ripping people off. Was anything you told her true?" he asked.

"Yeah, I am getting divorced, but we've been separated for about two years now. He's a right nasty bastard, so yeah, that part is true. But Becks, Jesus, she's so drone, beyond boring, it's no wonder you came looking for me. All I needed to do was tell her there was a child involved and she jumped at the chance to be the hero, she's utterly ridiculous. So, anyway, that part aside, the money, two thousand pounds by tomorrow or I'll tell her everything," Suzy said confidently.

"I never came looking for you, you've played the pair of us, and look at you, so pleased with yourself. I can't get cash just like that, Becks can see all the accounts. Please, Suzy, please, I beg you, don't do this," he pleaded.

"Come on, Becks told me what a whizz you are with numbers. She stood here in this house, bragging about how wonderful you are. So, show me, play with those figures, like you played with me, surely you can take it from your business, right? The wonderful business your wife boasted about. That's the deal, take it or leave it," she said back to him, as she wiggled her phone in her right hand.

"Fine! I'll get you the cash. I'll get it to you by tomorrow. I can't do anything online but, promise me, once I give you this money, you'll delete those images?" Connor asked.

"Why would I do that? So you can pay once and then not bother? This is my leverage. I want two thousand pounds every month, and don't be late," she replied. Exhausted and frustrated, Connor stepped out of his own house, feeling trapped and helpless. It was all because he'd foolishly allowed his pants to dictate his choices.

Upon returning to work at 12:10 pm, Margaret wasted no time in seeking out the latest gossip.

"So, what happened? Is everything sorted, Mr Jones?" she asked.

"No! No, it's far from sorted. Cancel my afternoon, I have to sort some figures out," Connor said, as he slammed his office door shut. He sat at his desk and delved into the spreadsheets, skilfully manoeuvring numbers to discreetly extract two thousand pounds. Carrying the company card, he strolled into town, confidently entering the bank to withdraw the sum in fifty-pound notes. However, as he made his way back to the office, a mix of anger, agitation, and self-reproach consumed him, leaving him feeling foolish. He sat daydreaming at his desk all afternoon, being very unproductive. As the clock struck 5 pm, he made his way back to his former residence.

He pressed the doorbell and, to his dislike, she appeared before him once more. Unafraid, she locked eyes with him, unyielding and resolute.

"Here," Connor said, as he handed her the brown envelope.

"See, I knew you could do it. That was quicker than I thought it would be, too. Thanks, same again on 1 June, don't forget," she said.

"The 1 June? That's less than two weeks away, I can't get it by then," Connor expressed.

"Well, you have to," Suzy replied.

"I'll try my best, but you better keep your fucking mouth shut and pay that as rent to Becks by Friday," he exclaimed as he moved closer to her, extending his finger towards her face.

"Oh, I love it when you're forceful. See you on 1 June, can't wait," she said, as she smiled and waved at him playfully.

Frustrated, he slammed the front door behind him, and raced home, taking each turn with haste. Upon arrival, he swiftly entered his house, where Becks awaited him as usual.

"No gym tonight?" she asked.

"No, I've had a shitty day," he replied.

"And half of that is my fault, I'm so sorry," Becks replied, as she stirred the boiling pan on the hob.

"No, no it's not you, just an issue at work, don't worry, please. How was your day?" he asked.

"I feel awful, I can't concentrate. I'm so sorry, I've messed everything up," Becks replied.

"You haven't at all, it's a simple mistake to make, you trusted her. She'll pay, I'm sure of it," he replied, in an attempt to comfort her. "I'm going to freshen up and change before dinner," Connor said to Becks, as he ran up the stairs.

In a rush, Connor made his way to his office, retrieving the meticulously organised file that Becks had prepared containing all the rental documents. As he sifted through the papers, he found Kerry's passport copy. Glancing at her photo and then at her name caused a wave of horror to wash over him. Scrunching the document tightly in his hand, he could feel the anger building up inside. Just then, Becks called out, "Dinner's ready."

Connor managed to smooth out the crumpled paper and discreetly placed it beneath the other documents before returning the file to its designated spot in the cupboard. He then proceeded to his room, washed his face, changed his clothes, and joined his family for dinner, all the while simmering with anger.

The following day, Becks reviewed her bank account only to find that the money had not been deposited. By Thursday, there was still no indication of the rent payment, causing her to feel anxious once more.

"Has the money gone in?" Connor asked.

"No, she has until tomorrow," Becks replied.

"She'll pay, try not to worry," he said confidently.

Friday morning arrived, but the money was nowhere in sight. Becks and Connor went about their usual work routine, with Becks anxiously checking every hour for any sign of the payment. However, as the day progressed, there was still no trace of it. Then, at 4:30 pm, Connor called Becks.

"Hi love, are you OK? Anything?" he asked.

"No, I'm going to ring the solicitor, as the eviction notice can be put in place from tomorrow morning. Let's get that ball rolling. Whatever she's doing, she's making us sweat. What a vile specimen she is, how could she do this to us? How do people live with themselves?" Becks replied.

"I know. There are just people like this in the world, Becks, a waste of oxygen, and we, the hard-working ones, end up paying for their laziness," Connor said supportively. Filled with a mix of anger and frustration, he yearned for Suzy to face the consequences of her actions. However, amidst his emotions, a sense of fear crept in, leaving him feeling utterly powerless and overwhelmed by the harsh reality of the situation.

At 4:45 pm, Connor left the office for what should have been a relaxing weekend. Instead, he headed towards the old house. He parked his car on the driveway, then pressed the doorbell.

With his top button undone and his tie slightly askew, he appeared both frustrated and exhausted.

"Well, hello, back again so soon?" Suzy answered, wearing a short skirt, large heels and a boob-tube-style top. He looked at her with disgust.

"What the hell are you playing at?" Connor said in anger, as he barged past her again.

"Excuse me, tenant's rights, you can't just barge in here," Suzy replied.

"I can when the tenant is blackmailing the landlord. Where's the money and why haven't you paid the rent?" Connor asked in pure rage.

"Well, I was going to but I got my head turned by a new handbag, and then, of course, I needed a facial. I got my hair and nails done yesterday, too. How do I look?" she said, as she posed for him.

"You spent it?" Connor asked, exhaling deeply. The expression on his face betrayed his disbelief, as though he couldn't fathom what was happening.

"Yeah, but if you get me more, I'll pay you the rent. Well, your wife. I know you're going to evict me anyway, so I thought, who cares," Suzy replied.

"You're not getting another penny from me, you deluded little bitch," he said, with fury in his eyes.

"Fine, then say bye-bye to your family," she said with a smirk on her face, holding up her phone.

"You're the most twisted little twat I've ever come across. How fucking dare you do this to us?" Connor retorted furiously.

"Connor, this was all your own doing. You're so bored with that dull woman of yours. You needed me, you needed the excitement. I saw you. I saw how your eyes lit up when you saw me, and I also saw how they rolled back in your head when you were inside me. Your wife doesn't do that to you," Suzy said, pouting.

"Don't even say her name, you're not worthy of that. She's one hundred times the woman you'll ever be. You're disgusting. A dirty, dirty slut, who does nothing but fuck men to get along in life," he said, rage burning in his eyes as he expressed his emotions.

This level of anger was completely new to him, overwhelming his senses like never before.

"Oh, Connor, if I'm that useless and that stupid, then how have I managed for three months to live here rent-free, seduce you and get two grand out of you? You two were ridiculously easy to play, one of the easiest if I'm honest. And you. You were that desperate to have some fun and loosen that top button of yours, you loved it. You loved every damn minute of being with me, but you're just too fucking scared to admit it, because then you'll realise how dull your life is," Suzy replied, as she went close and put her finger on his nose playfully. He hit her hand away.

"Suzy, I'm not joking, give me my money and get the fuck out of my house. Actually, do you know what? Keep the God damn money. Just get out. Leave now and I won't say another word. Pack your things and go," Connor exclaimed in a fit of rage. He closed in on her, his large hand firmly gripping her chin.

Suzy began to laugh. "And why would I do that? I have you by the balls, not for the first time I might add, and you loved it the first time. I'm not going anywhere. If you want to keep your wife and your kids, I wouldn't be threatening me again, do you understand me? One press, just one button and these pictures can be sent to her," Suzy said. She pushed his hand away, her gaze locked onto him, her eyes piercing into his soul as she held her phone firmly in her right hand.

His blood was boiling.

"Give me that fucking phone!" he shouted, as he drove himself towards her, pushing her back through the lounge door.

"There, there he is, come on big boy – show me what you've got. I know you want me, you want this," Suzy said.

"I want nothing to do with you!" he shouted with a loud cry. At that moment, he forcefully shoved her aside using his left hand and reached out with his right hand to snatch the phone. As a result, Suzy stumbled backwards, struggling to maintain her balance in her towering six-inch heels.

As she fell, he shouted, "GIVE ME IT NOW!"

Suzy's body plummeted backwards, crashing onto the fragile glass table with a resounding shatter. In a horrifying twist of fate, she found herself impaled by a gleaming golden spike that had pierced through her from behind, emerging out the front of her body.

"Suzy?" Connor shouted, with a look of horror on his face. Her gaze fixated on the spike piercing through her abdomen. With a grimace, she raised her arms towards the sharp spike protruding from her abdomen and then turned her horrified eyes towards him. In an instant, her body went limp, her arms dropping to her sides as her phone slipped from her grasp and landed on the rug. Blood seeped out, staining the cream shag pile.

Connor panicked; he was unable to comprehend what had just occurred.

"Suzy?" he said, as he felt for a pulse in her neck. She'd gone white, lifeless, she'd stopped breathing.

"Shit! Shit! No, no, no!" he shouted over and over, putting his hands over his face. In a rush, he sprinted towards the downstairs toilet, desperately grabbing a handful of towels to absorb the bloodstains. Trembling with fear, he carefully manoeuvred his hands, determined not to stain his clothes with the crimson liquid.

In a moment of despair, he sank into the sofa, his hands shielding his face while she lay, motionless, impaled by the table's stake. Overwhelmed by uncertainty, he rose and paced back and forth, his hands repeatedly caressing his face. There was only one person he could confide in but now he knew that his actions would shatter that bond, and the burden of truth would weigh heavily upon him.

Retrieving his phone from his pocket, he dialled Becks' number and patiently waited for her to pick up. With a sense of resolve, he accepted that he had no other option but to confront his punishment head on.

"Hello," Becks answered.

"Where are you?" Connor's voice trembled with panic.

"At home, why, where are you?" she answered.

"I need you. Please, don't ask any questions. Listen carefully, I need you to drop the boys off with the neighbour and come to the old house. Don't park on the drive, drive into the estate, pull up outside Petal Lane – there are no cameras there – and walk down the hill," Connor said.

"What are you talking about?" Becks asked.

"Please, no questions, just do as I ask. Please, don't bring the boys, just come as soon as you can to the house, please," Connor requested.

Becks gathered her wits and, in a hurry, entrusted the boys to Janet, their neighbour, and sped off as fast as she could, feeling as if the four-mile distance had suddenly stretched out endlessly. Following his instructions, she parked her car on the side of the road and hurriedly made her way down the hill to the house, only to discover Kerry's car already parked there, with Connor's car right behind hers.

As she reached out to press the doorbell she hesitated, then Connor swiftly swung the door open and ushered her inside. Without wasting a moment, he secured the door with a lock and chain, ensuring their privacy and safety.

"What on earth is going on, why are you here?" Becks asked. The perplexity in her eyes was evident, as she grappled with the jumble of thoughts swirling in her mind.

"OK, I ask you, please, to stay composed. Assure me, please, that you'll remain calm, and I promise, Becks, I'll do what you request of me," Connor said.

"You're scaring me," Becks said, as Connor opened the living room door.

"Please, stay calm," Connor repeated.

"Oh my God!" Becks shouted, as she covered her mouth, closed her eyes and turned to look away. Catching a glimpse, she was petrified by the haunting image of Kerry's impaled body on the stake. It sent a shiver down her spine.

"No! No! No! What the hell has happened, did you do this?" she asked, as she took a deep breath and screamed out.

"Becks, I didn't do this, it was an accident, I swear, it was an accident. Please, you need to be quiet," Connor replied, grabbing both her arms in an attempt to calm her.

"You better start talking," Becks threatened.

Connor led her into the kitchen, while Kerry's lifeless body remained in the living room.

"I don't even know where to start Becks, just please hear me out before you react," he said.

"Do you know her?" Becks asked.

"Yes, well, not at first, and I didn't know she was our tenant. In January, she came to the gym and she started talking to me, flirting with me and, at first, I must admit, I was flattered. She was pretty and forward and I felt humbled by the attention she was giving me," he continued.

"Please, tell me you didn't have an affair with this woman?" Becks asked, confused.

"I'm sorry Becks, I'm so, so sorry," he cried, as he put his head down.

"For fuck's sake! You? You had an affair? You're the perfect husband and father, you're safe, how could you do this?" Becks asked.

"Please, listen to me. It wasn't an affair, she planned all of this. She admitted it, she told me that she saw your profile, she saw you were married to me, clicked on my profile and, apparently, I looked easy, gullible," he said, as he flung his hands in the air.

"Connor!" Becks said. Sorrow and confusion shrouded her face.

"She planned this entire thing, Becks. I only knew it was her when she walked into court. She gave me a fake name and created a fake profile. I knew her as Suzy, not Kerry. She knew who I was, she'd done her research and she targeted me," he said, embracing the role of a genuine sufferer.

"So how did it end up like this? She's dead!" Becks exclaimed.

"She was blackmailing me. After court, she knew I would come to see her, to confront her, which I did. She then told me that I had to give her two thousand pounds a month to pay the rent otherwise she would tell you everything," he said.

"I wouldn't have believed her," Becks replied.

"She had pictures of me, so you would have," he replied sheepishly.

"Pictures? Pictures of what? How far did this go? Did you sleep with her?" Becks asked.

"I'm not going to lie to you Becks, I promise, everything I'm telling you is the truth but you have to promise not to act in anger, please. Yes, yes, I slept with her, it was stupid, I was an idiot for falling into her trap," he said.

"Jesus, how many times? Where? Was she in our house?" Becks continued asking questions.

"Can we not go into the details right now? We need to decide what we're going to do," he asked.

"So that's a yes then, you shagged this woman, this con artist, in our house? And there was me feeling terrible about what I did!" Becks said in anger.

"What do you want me to do? Shall I call the police now? I'll go to prison, Becks, when they investigate this. I have a motive, there's no way I can call this self-defence, but if that's what you want me to do, then I'll do it," Connor said. Connor's expression was a mix of puppy dog eyes and a frown, conveying his sadness.

"And I suppose you want me to decide right now?" Becks asked.

"The problem is, we don't have much time. I either need to call them now, or we have to move her body," he replied.

"Move her body! This isn't a film, you're a God damn accountant, I'm a school teacher. You're not Eastenders answer to the next Phil Mitchell, have you heard yourself talk?" Becks exclaimed sharply.

"OK, then I have to call them. We have no other choice," he replied.

"Fuck! Fuck! I could kill you right now," she said back in haste. She seldom uttered curse words, however she found herself unable to resist in this particular situation.

"Becks, I understand, I understand completely, I've betrayed you, I've let you and our boys down and I'm sorry, I'm so, so sorry," Connor said, as he attempted to come towards her.

"Don't come near me. You do realise you're jeopardising me in this, you're adding me to your crime?" Becks replied.

"It was an accident. This isn't me, I'm not aggressive, she just pissed me off, and she fell backwards as I tried to get her phone out of her hand," he replied.

"Did you give her money?" Becks asked sharply.

"Yes, I gave her two thousand pounds after court on Monday. She said she'd pay you but she never did, hence why I came over today to try and convince her to leave or pay you, but she wasn't doing either," Connor said in desperation.

Becks paused for a minute, deep in thought.

"I don't want you to call the police, but don't for one minute think it's for your sake, you could rot for all I care. But the boys, oh my goodness, our innocent little boys, I can't have their father taken away because of a stupid accident that was conspired by this evil woman. I'll help you, but we need to be thorough, we need to figure this out step by step," Becks said logically. Despite her initial reluctance and fear, she understood the urgency and importance of taking swift and decisive action. However, hidden beneath her calm exterior, a whirlwind of fear, rage, and sorrow consumed her.

While deep in conversation, Kerry's phone suddenly rang, causing both of them to pause, exchange glances, and then head into the living room.

"Darcy's calling. That's her daughter, what do we do?" Becks asked.

"I don't know, we can't answer it, just let it ring out," Connor replied.

"What if she comes home?" Becks asked.

"We'll deal with that if it happens," Connor said. He exuded an air of tranquillity and composure now, knowing that he wasn't going to call the police.

"The patio. The patio slabs. Most of them are broken, I say we pull them up, dig a hole, put her body in there and then concrete and slab over her," Connor suggested.

"Do you think?" Becks asked.

"Do you have any other suggestions?" Connor asked.

"No, I guess not, we can't move her far," Becks replied.

"OK, you go home and get the tarpaulin from the garage, you know, the one we used for the boys' water slide last year, get any bits of rope, parcel tape, a shovel and as many bags of cement that we have in the garage. Unless you want me to go? I'll check to see if there's a shovel in the garage here and start digging?" Connor said, his words rapidly leaving his mouth.

"I don't know. I don't want to go and leave you, and I don't want to be left here with her, either," Becks said.

"We can't both go, if anyone comes over then we're screwed," Connor said.

"You go, you'll be quicker than me. I'll start bagging her belongings. We also need to send me a message from her phone asking me to come over. This way, if there's a missing person report they'll surely question us and we can say that she agreed to leave," Becks said methodically.

"Good plan. OK, I'll be twenty minutes, we'll do that when I get back. Thank you for this, I'm so sorry," Connor said quietly and quickly in a panic.

Becks chose not to respond and instead took the lead, walking ahead of Connor towards the front door. She opened the door and made sure to lock it behind him. As she turned back, she made a conscious effort to disregard the gruesome sight of the impaled dead body. Closing the lounge door, she proceeded to the kitchen, where she retrieved bin bags from the under-sink cupboard to attend to her task. She then walked upstairs and stuffed as many clothes as she could into the bags. In a flash, she began emptying the drawers. Surprisingly, the woman didn't possess many personal belongings, as the house had been left fully furnished by Connor and Becks. This made the process quick and efficient for her. However, when she reached the room belonging to Kerry's daughter, her heart sank. It was a poignant sight, a little girl's bedroom. The realisation hit her hard, a young girl was now without her mother.

Despite the heaviness in her chest, she pressed on fearlessly, carefully packing everything into bags. Each item she stored away only fuelled her frustration, causing her anger to grow with every moment. The child's possessions were now packed into five bin bags. As she removed the pictures from the walls, those innocent snapshots, she saw a little girl sitting beside the evil woman who had just shattered their lives.

Laden with bags, she descended the stairs, her weary legs and heavy heart weighing her down. She continuously traversed the stairs multiple times, her mind consumed with thoughts. Finally, she deposited all the bags in the hallway before making her way through the kitchen towards the backyard.

Pausing for a moment, her gaze fell upon the shattered slabs that once formed a cherished patio where her children had frolicked. Without any hesitation, she began to lift and remove the broken pieces, symbolically erasing the memories of her little ones' joyful footsteps. As she yanked each one, her strength grew, and she forcefully slammed them onto the ground until they broke apart. It felt cathartic, a release of pent-up frustration.

Without warning, Connor reappeared via the side gate, catching Becks in the act of lifting the slabs.
"I'll do that," he said, as he walked towards her.
With a swipe of her arm, she cleared the sweat off her forehead before giving her reply, "It's fine, it's very therapeutic. Every time I throw one, I think it's your head!"
"Becks," Connor said as he looked at her.
"Now is not the time. This needs to be done now, and quickly!" she exclaimed.
He grabbed the tarpaulin, rope, shovel, and cement from the boot of his car, sneaking into the garden through the side gate to avoid being seen before locking the back gate securely. With his assistance, the slabs were lifted rapidly and within minutes the area was clear. They stood and looked at each other.
"Are you sure about this?" Connor asked.
"No, no I'm not, but what other choice do we have?" Becks asked.
Connor gazed at her before starting to dig. His time spent at the gym was paying off, with his impressive upper body strength making him resemble a modern-day caveman.

Becks couldn't help but feel the weight of reality sinking in as the hole grew deeper. Her gaze shifted downwards, fixating on Connor's figure deep inside the crater.

"OK, I think this should be deep enough," Connor said, as he looked up at Becks.

"I don't know if I can do this." Shock registered on Becks' face as she uttered the words.

"It's too late, we can't go back now, please. We're lucky that the garden isn't overlooked," Connor said, jokingly.

"What's wrong with you? This is not the time to make jokes. Have you stopped to think about what we're doing?" Becks replied.

"I'm sorry, I know, but this is our only option. Come on, let's get her wrapped up," Connor said quietly, but yet so confidently.

"Do you think we can manage to lift her?" Becks asked.

"She's small, she doesn't weigh anything. We can do this, together we can do it," Connor replied positively.

"So, you've lifted her then? Jesus, when we finish here, I want to know everything, I mean it!" Becks exclaimed. Her anger towards him was palpable.

Connor looked at her in sorrow. "I promise, I'll explain everything, I will," he replied.

Returning to the living room, seeing the lifeless body pierced in a gruesome manner, Becks inhaled deeply and prepared herself for what lay ahead. Connor carefully stretched the tarpaulin on the ground meticulously.

"OK, I'll get her top half, you grab her legs and, on three, we lift her off the spike and lay her on the tarpaulin," Connor said, confidently.

"OK," Becks agreed.

"Are you ready? One, two, three, lift!" Connor said loudly.

As they pried her off the stake, the sound of it piercing through her flesh and exiting her body, coupled with the unsettling motion of her body being lifted, made Becks' stomach turn.

"Oh my God, I can't!" Becks screamed.

"It's OK, don't let go, she's off, she's off, you did it, well done. Now, move over onto the tarpaulin," he said, as they held her body in the air.

"Don't let go, lay her down, that's it, you did great," Connor's words came out in a rush, as he desperately tried to catch his breath.

"OK, I won't," Becks replied.

"Now, let's wrap her, then we need to wrap the rug around her too, we can then carry her out of the patio doors and into the hole. The table spike needs to go on top of her in there," he said firmly.

They wrapped her body in the plush, cream shag pile carpet stained with blood and fragments of glass from the shattered table. Then, the additional tarpaulin was wrapped around the waterproof backing, secured with rope and tape in four spots, creating a scene reminiscent of a movie straight from television.

"That should be secure. Right, this is the last big move, it will be heavier, but I know you can do this," Connor said encouragingly.

"I'm using all my hatred for you right now. I hate you for putting me through this!" she exclaimed.

"I know, I know, I'm so sorry. On three again, are you ready?" he replied.

"Yes, I think so," she said, as she adjusted her hands to get a better grip.

"Right, one, two, three, lift!" he said, as they lifted Kerry's wrapped up body into the air.

They had managed it, the rug was lifted and carried out through the back patio doors before her body was tossed into the hole like a discarded pair of worn out trainers, landing with a thud. Connor then re-entered the living room to retrieve the spike and threw it on top of her with zero remorse, sending a shiver down Becks' spine as the spike hit the rug.

"Right, let's throw the towels and then the broken slabs, this will act like hardcore, then I need to put the mud back. You go and see the living room carpet, look if any blood has seeped through. I've got us some spare clothes too, we need to change and make sure there's no blood on us," he said. His words tumbled out faster with each sentence, a clear sign of his escalating panic.

"You've thought of everything, haven't you?" Becks replied in utter dismay. She'd never imagined that one day she would have to dispose of a body in such a horrific manner. Connor felt a mix of exhaustion and disbelief as he started replacing the mud. Drenched in sweat and covered in dirt, his emotions ran high as adrenaline fuelled his every move.

Returning to the living room, Becks was relieved to find that the waterproof backing on the faux shag pile rug had prevented any blood from seeping onto the carpet. It was the first moment of relief she'd experienced all evening.

Connor returned the mud to its original place before incorporating a generous amount of sand. With utmost care, he firmly pressed it down, ensuring its solidity to the best of his ability.

"That should do it, now I need to put a layer of concrete on top. I'll lay new slabs on Sunday. Help me mix this, please," he said to Becks, as he picked up a bag of cement. He was out of breath, tired and weary.

With each bag they emptied into the worn out bucket, their fatigue grew. In the dim light, he skilfully poured and smoothed the concrete using an old piece of wood, doing his best to level it perfectly.

"That should be OK. I'll put these in the garage for now. We need a skip here on Monday to get rid of all this, can you call them tomorrow?" Connor asked.

"Yes, yes, I will," Becks replied.

"We need to make it look like she's moving out to the neighbours, we don't want anything being said to anyone about this," Connor said.

"OK, so what next?" Becks asked.

"So, tomorrow, we come back and we get rid of her car. Did you find any documents while you were packing her stuff up?" Connor asked.

"Yes, I've put them all in a box, it's in the kitchen. Passport, purse, car documents, bank statements, she had money coming in from all over, how did I fall for this?" Becks said, with a solemn look on her face.

"We both fell for this; she was good at what she did. She was a criminal, a professional," Connor said.

He walked into the kitchen and searched inside the old shoe box.

"Here's the car document, it's in a man's name, Michael Reed, I'm guessing it's her husband? What do you think?" Connor asked.

"Yes, I guess so. How are we going to get rid of it?" Becks asked.

"We go onto her phone and do a Cash Car quote, there's one on that industrial estate a few miles down the road. We do it from here, on her phone, and we book the appointment for tomorrow night. I'll set up an email in her husband's name and permit her to sell the car. Look, she has a copy of his passport, this is perfect, we can use this as his ID," Connor said energetically.

"You're forgetting one thing, who's going to drop this car off?" Becks asked. As he looked at her, a slight smile tugged at the corners of his mouth.

"That's where you come in, Becks. You need to wear a baseball cap, those ridiculous big glasses that she wears, the tight leggings, and turn on your charm. Then, you need to get a taxi back to this area and get out of the taxi where the cameras stop, in case they ever follow up her trail," Connor said.

"You're out of your mind if you think I'm doing that. And, you seem to know this woman very well, don't you!" Becks said sarcastically.

"I—" Connor began to speak, but was interrupted.

"I'm not dressing up in a dead woman's clothes and pretending to be her, you're crazy!" Becks said.

"Please, this is the only way. If we take it anywhere else it will look suspicious, this way they can see her active after she left here," Connor replied.

"But she won't be leaving us, will she? This is crazy, I can't pull that off, I just can't, I'm sorry," Becks replied.

"Becks, listen, you can do this, you're similar builds, you have blonde hair. Keep the glasses on, tell them you suffer from headaches, you can put loads of makeup on and they won't notice, trust me," Connor explained.

"Trust you! Those words coming out of your mouth!" Becks thought for a second, but there was no other way.

"I'll do it. But I mean it, if I get in any trouble, I'll never forgive you, ever," Becks said.

"I appreciate what you're doing for me, I don't deserve this. You're an amazing woman," Connor uttered, to boost his wife's morale and uplift her spirits.

"This is far from over. If you think I've forgiven you, even remotely, you're mistaken. I'm doing this for our boys, they don't deserve to have their daddy taken away for something that you didn't mean to do. But know this, you've let them down. You're their father, and you've let our boys down!" she repeated in anger.

Connor grabbed Kerry's phone, entered the password and, just like that, they were granted entry.

"You know her passcode?" Becks asked, a look of disbelief on her face.

"She didn't tell me her passcode; I saw her type it in when she showed me the pictures. You know me and numbers, I remembered it, that's all, I promise," he casually remarked. He appeared utterly unconcerned whether she believed him or not.

"Whatever, send me a text asking me to come over, write it like she wrote the others to me. Say that she's sorry and that she'll be moving out tomorrow. Make sure to say that she'd like to see me to give me the keys and apologise in person. Make it at least look authentic," Becks explained.

"OK, I've sent it. Please, check it's come to you?" Connor replied.

"Yes, it's here," Becks confirmed.

"Read it now," he replied.

"No, I need to read it away from this house, the police could track my phone. I'll read it when we get back home. We have to get our story straight on this, too," Becks said nervously. Anxiety consumed her. She was fearful of the repercussions that could arise and potentially lead to trouble for them.

"We will, let's just sort this first," he replied, as he started scrolling through Kerry's phone.

"What are you doing?" Becks asked.

"I'm just looking at the other messages, there are loads of people," Connor replied, his face showing utter embarrassment and shame. As he scrolled, Kerry's phone began to ring again.

"It's Darcy again," Connor said, holding the phone up to show Becks.

"What if she was meant to pick her up," Becks said. It stopped ringing and then beeped to show a voice message.

"She's left a voicemail," Connor said.

As soon as he hit the play button, Darcy's voice began to speak.

"Mum, where are you? I've called like three times. Anyway, I'm at Dad's house, he'll drop me back on Sunday, love ya," Becks was horrified when she heard the voice of the young girl. Her face filled with sorrow. This poor, innocent girl remained unaware of the situation that had just unfolded. However, it was a relief to know that Darcy wouldn't be back at the house until Sunday. The anticipation of her absence brought a sense of calm and peace.

"So at least she's not due back here. That's a huge relief," Connor said, thanking his lucky stars.

"Are we just going to let her walk into an empty house?" Becks asked.

"We have to. I might be here, anyway. I'll be laying the new patio. I can tell her that she's moved out, don't worry," Connor supportively said.

"How can I not worry? This little girl has lost her mum, she has no idea and she won't know, she'll think she just abandoned her," Becks exclaimed. She was scared and concerned. This could all go wrong.

"You need to calm down, please, we still have a lot to do," Connor said. As he went to touch her arm, she flinched and quickly pulled her arm away.

"Can you at least send Darcy a text, just say that she loves her or something?" Becks asked.

"Why don't you type it. What do the other messages say?" Connor asked.

"I'll type it," Becks replied, as she held out her hand to ensure he didn't come any closer.

"Don't say anything about moving," Connor replied.

"I won't, I'm not stupid. How about, 'Hi, sweetheart, have a lovely time, love you.' There, it's sent. I feel better knowing that there's a little warmth for that poor child. What's next?" Becks asked, as she returned the phone to Connor.

"The car. I'll request a quote now and accept it. If I book the appointment for tomorrow night, we need to stage her leaving. I then need to create an email account on this phone for her husband to give permission. You need to take her driving licence, a bank statement and a copy of his passport with you, that should be enough. I've done a few of these for clients previously," he said confidently.

"What if there's finance outstanding?" she asked.

"Shit, I didn't think of that. Did you see any papers?" he replied.

"No, but the car is in his name," she answered.

"We have to try, just say no if they ask," he replied.

Connor obtained a car quote, stumbled upon a bank statement, jotted down the bank information, and scheduled the car drop off for 6 pm the next day. He proceeded to set up a fake email account in Michael Reed's name and sent Cash Car a message authorising his wife to deliver the vehicle.

"I can't think of anything else. I'll put her licence and the bank details together, along with his passport. You need her phone, too, then when you get out of the taxi, take out the sim, cut it up and bin it," he said.

"I have a really bad feeling about this," Becks said, nervously.

"You can do this, you can. I'm so grateful, Becks, I am," he replied. Lost in contemplation, he yearned for flawlessness, leaving no room for error, aware that any slip up could lead to a lifetime behind bars if they were discovered.

Connor then decided to make a bold move. Using her credit card, he booked a one way ticket to Majorca. With Kerry's passport in hand, he aimed to create the illusion that she'd left the country. Returning to her phone, he selected a Sunday morning flight and, just like that, an email confirmation appeared. The time had come to bid farewell to Suzy.

"Why have you done that?" Becks asked.

"There needs to be a trail, it needs to look like she had a plan, selling the car and fleeing the country," he said.

"I'm guessing we discard all of this paperwork tomorrow?" she asked.

"Yes, once the car has gone, we'll shred the papers, burn the passport and cut up the cards. We just need to keep our cool, the hardest part is over," he said.

Connor opened the app where they'd been communicating. As he scrolled through numerous messages from different men, he eventually found his name. Upon reviewing their communication, he was relieved to see that he'd never sent her any inappropriate messages. The only messages from him were asking her to stop contacting him. He erased his messages, navigated to the trash folder, and permanently deleted them. In addition, he removed several more, aiming to be prepared for any potential inquiries by thinking creatively.

With the bin bags in tow, they made their way to Connor's car, ready to dispose of them at a nearby charity clothing bin. However, before doing so, Becks managed to find the ideal Kerry-style ensemble from one of the bags, ensuring she looked her best for her final task. Becks made sure to close all the curtains on both floors of the house and left the hallway light on to give the impression that there was someone inside.

After changing their clothes, they neatly packed the soiled garments into a separate black bin bag. Taking care of every detail, they diligently wiped down each door handle before exiting through the back door and securing the house. Becks quickly hopped into the back of Connor's car, making sure to keep a low profile and he subsequently drove her to her vehicle.

The previous hours seemed to exist in a parallel dimension, where time passed at an accelerated pace and their actions and words appeared to occur at twice the speed.

"I'll just drop these clothes at the charity bins and I'll be home," he said. Becks jumped into her car and headed straight back to their luxurious estate. She collected the boys, and expressed her heartfelt gratitude to her neighbour for coming to their aid on such short notice.

As they walked through their front door, she was drained and worn out. She yearned for a moment of rest to alleviate her tiredness. However, her children, as per usual, were bursting with their customary liveliness.

"Boys, straight into pyjamas tonight, we'll have a bath tomorrow, OK?" Becks said to them. The boys eagerly ran upstairs.

"OK, Mummy," Rory shouted.

"Boys, no messing, pyjamas on and brush your teeth, please, it's late," Becks shouted up the stairs. After successfully tucking them into bed, she eagerly awaited Connor's return from dropping off Kerry's clothes.

Upon seeing the heartfelt message from Kerry, that Connor had fabricated, she stopped and read it to herself in a whispering voice.

'Hi hun, I can only apologise to you, you were so kind to me, giving me the keys to your beautiful house, and I took advantage. I'm sorry for not paying you the rent, but I just couldn't afford it with the divorce. I'm leaving tomorrow. Could you come over at 5 pm tomorrow? I'll have all my things packed and will give you your keys back. I'm sorry honey xxx.' In that moment, she had a sudden realisation of her husband's manipulative nature, his skilful deceit became apparent to her. Becks struggled to contain her emotions and her hands began to shake as she started to respond.

'Hi Kerry, I won't lie, it's been a very stressful time for us. However, if you leave tomorrow as you say, then we'll not say any more about it. We won't chase you for the remaining funds and will drop the court proceedings against you. I'll see you at 5 pm tomorrow. Becks.' Her fingers trembled as she hit send, a wave of emotions washing over her.

Feeling a mix of guilt and regret, she sought solace in the shower, standing under the running water and questioning her actions. Images of Kerry haunted her thoughts, causing her heart to race and her anxiety to spike. As she stood under the shower washing away the shampoo from her hair, a wave of guilt washed over her, leaving her feeling shattered and betrayed. She couldn't help but wonder where they had gone astray. Overwhelmed by emotions, she collapsed to the floor, tears mingling with the cascading water as she let out a heart-wrenching cry.

Connor returned home while Becks was showering, still in a focused state. He proceeded to open the garage door, store the shovel, dispose of the empty concrete bags, and place the bag of clothes in the garage. Carrying Kerry's documents, which included the final outfit, he concealed the box in the cupboard beneath the stairs.

He tossed his keys aside, took off his shoes, and walked slowly up the stairs to discover Becks, sitting and cradling her knees on the shower floor.

"Becks?" he exclaimed, as he ran towards her. He got into the shower fully clothed and held her.

"Get away from me, how dare you do this, how fucking dare you!" she shouted.

"It was all a huge mistake, the biggest mistake I've ever made. I was weak, I let myself be lured in and she took advantage of me," he replied in desperation.

"Don't do that. Don't put the blame all on her. Yes, she was wrong, but you, you knew better. You have a wife, a family, why? Why did you do that?" she asked.

"I have no answers for you," he replied, as he stood in the shower, his clothes seeped in water.

"Just get out," Becks said.

"Out where, Becks? Do you want me to leave the house?" he asked.

"Well, you can't can you? We still have to go tomorrow to sort this bloody car out," she replied.

"Do you mind if I have a shower?" he asked quietly.

"Knock yourself out," she replied, as she stood up, opened the shower door, wrapped herself in a towel, and left him in the bathroom.

Connor stripped off his damp clothes, threw them into the laundry basket, and scrubbed himself clean, making sure to scrub away the grime from under his fingernails. Despite feeling scared and anxious – his hands were trembling – he knew he had to stay strong.

After stepping out of the shower he made his way to the bedroom, where Becks was sitting up in the bed, clad in her cosy pyjamas, her damp hair neatly tucked into a towel. He quickly changed into his pyjamas and perched himself nervously on the edge of the bed. A wave of uncertainty washed over him as he grappled with the unfamiliarity of the situation, unsure of how to conduct himself in her presence, leaving him feeling uneasy.

"Becks," he said quietly.

"You can sleep in the spare room tonight, I can't have you near me," Becks said.

"I understand. Can we talk, please?" Connor asked desperately.

"Yes, yes, OK, let's talk. Where shall we begin? How about the affair you had – the fact you slept with another woman and lied to me for weeks? The fact that the same woman is now dead and buried under the patio in our rental?" Her emotions took hold, causing her voice to intensify.

"Please, love," Connor repeated.

"Jesus Christ, this is surreal. How have we just done that? We're a normal family, simple people, this is absurd!" she exclaimed.

"I have no excuses and I have no answers. I'm so sorry. I'm a weak man, a stupid man, I had no self-control and I wish I could go back in time. It was a stupid, stupid mistake. I didn't have feelings for her, it just happened," he replied, in an attempt to plead his case.

"Just happened? Tell me how many times it 'just happened', and where. I want to know everything, and don't even try to say it was a mistake, because a mistake is forgetting an appointment or picking up the wrong brand of cereal. Having sex with someone else when you're married is not a mistake, it's selfish, it's wrong and it's all your fault," she replied angrily.

"You're right, which is why I'm owning up to it, I'm being truthful. I was weak. It's shameful, and my behaviour was selfish and wrong," he agreed.

"So, tell me, tell me when this started. How many times?" she asked, with a disgusted look on her face.

"It was three times, that's all," Connor said, as Becks cut in.

"That's all? That's all! My God, you slept with her three times?" Shock and disbelief washed over her as she processed the words that had just reached her ears.

The sheer disgust she felt towards him was overwhelming, leaving her speechless and unable to comprehend the situation.

"And where did these three times occur?" Becks questioned.

"Once at the gym, which came as a complete surprise. I'd finished my workout, I got in the shower, and she followed me. I turned around and she was there, standing in the shower cubical, and I cracked. I was thinking with my pants and not my head, I regretted it immediately," he said.

"In the shower? Are you serious?" Becks asked, surprised and feeling so deeply hurt. He lowered his head in shame.

"I'm sorry," he repeated once again.

"And the second time?" Becks asked.

"In a hotel. She messaged me asking to meet her there. I said no, but she kept messaging and messaging so I went there to tell her to stop and when I walked in, she pounced on me. Again, it was wrong, I felt awful, sick," he answered.

"When was this Conor?" she asked.

"That Friday, when your dad had his heart attack. I fell asleep in the hotel, and she left. She closed the curtains and left me sleeping. That's when she took the pictures of me, and that's why I didn't hear your calls," he replied.

"You didn't hear my calls because you were having sex with another woman! You're a pig! You're an absolute pig of a man!"

she exclaimed with force, slamming her hand down on the mattress.

"I'm sorry. As soon as I woke up, I called you and came home, then I drove straight to you," he replied.

"Oh, that's so good of you, thank you," she replied sarcastically.

"I don't deserve you. I don't deserve to have you, I know that, but I don't want us to finish this. I can't lose you," he pleaded.

"And the third time?" Becks asked. Beneath the surface, she was shattered, yet she refused to reveal her pain through her expression.

"The night I came back from your parents. You'd stayed. She got our address from my driving licence. I'd blocked her on social media so she came over to the house. She'd seen that you weren't home. I told her to leave, but she came onto me again and I couldn't say no, I didn't say no and I'm sorry. I should've said no," Connor said, as tears began to fall down his cheeks.

"Now you're crying, that's great. You make a catastrophic error and then sit there and cry. I bet you weren't crying when you were shagging her in our bed, this bed, the bed we sleep in. My God, I feel sick," Becks said with anger.

"It wasn't in our bed. It was on the sofa chair, downstairs in the living room. I would never do that in our bed. It was wrong, so, so wrong of me. I asked her to leave immediately and I didn't see her again after that. Well, until the court date," he said, as his fingers remained in a constant state of restlessness. He continued to fidget with them.

Becks wore a look of utter shock on her face, unable to comprehend the words that had just reached her ears.

"You'll never know how disappointed I am in you. I never, ever, thought that you would do something like this to us. I'm your wife, your wife, but I guess that means nothing to you," she said with melancholy.

"You and our boys are everything, you mean the world to me. I'm not going to lie, it was exciting, it was different. You and I, we'd gone stale, it was routine. I just got my head turned and I was weak, I can't apologise enough, please. You have to forgive me and believe me, please," he begged.

"We're stale, stale? Do you know how hard I worked to keep everything in this house going so you could take over the business? Do you have any idea how hard it is to get up every morning, to do the same thing over and over again? It's boring, but I continue. Every day I do my duty, I care for our children, I work a very high-powered job so we can afford to live this way. I drop off and I pick up so you can go to the gym and release your frustration. WHAT ABOUT MY FUCKING FRUSTRATION?" she shouted.

"Becks, please, I'm sorry. I'm sorry," he repeated. He remained seated, sobbing, with tears cascading down his face.

"And, to top it all off, after you sleep with her, you then go and kill the damn woman and expect me to help tidy it up. I'm a fool, a fool to have ever believed in you," she said, as she flicked her wet hair back through her fingers.

Her demeanour was always composed, never resorting to swearing or vulgar expressions. Nevertheless, the fury that consumed her was simply beyond her control.

"You're not a fool, you're the nicest person I know, the best person I know. No one would ever do what you've done for me this evening, no one. You were the only person I could trust," he said.

"I'm the only one foolish enough. Please, just go to the spare room, I can't talk about this anymore," she replied.

He stood up. "I love you, please, know how sorry I am," he said, walking towards the door. He paused to glance back at her, but she avoided his gaze. Exiting the bedroom, he peeked into the boys' rooms to find them fast asleep, unaware of their surroundings. Making his way to the spare room, he climbed into bed and lay there, wide awake, with only his thoughts haunting him.

Becks sat upright in bed, tears flowing freely down her cheeks, absently toying with her engagement and wedding bands, symbols of love, that had never left her finger since the day they were tenderly slipped on. She couldn't even consider the possibility of sleep because her mind was filled with illusions. Images of Kerry's face flashed before her eyes, the sound of her being lifted off the spike echoed in her mind, and the thought of Connor and Kerry together consumed her thoughts. Could she ever move past this? She curled up in a ball, gripping the blanket tightly for some sense of solace. With doubts swirling in her head, she pondered how she would accomplish the daunting task of unburdening herself of the car. A wave of weakness and instability washed over her, dampening her spirits. Eventually, exhaustion overtook her, and she slipped into a deep sleep, only after catching a glimpse of the clock striking 3 am.

The next morning, at 7 am, the boys came barging in.

"Mummy, where's Daddy?" Logan asked.

"I'm here, boys. Hi, are you both OK? I've missed you," he asked, hugging them tightly. Becks sat up feeling disorientated.

"Good morning, boys, did you sleep well?" Becks asked.

"Yes, we're hungry," Logan replied.

"How about Daddy makes breakfast?" Connor suggested.

"Yes, please," Rory answered.

"I'll be down in a minute," Becks said.

"Take your time, I'll watch them, have some rest," Connor replied, smiling at her. Despite her best efforts, she found it impossible to make eye contact with him, let alone offer a smile. After they departed from her room, Becks lay her head on the pillow, trying desperately to rest, however, she was overwhelmed by pure anxiety.

She got herself out of bed, put on her dressing gown, and walked downstairs to join them. Standing at the foot of the staircase, she eavesdropped on their animated conversation about football, captivated by the enthusiasm in their voices. In that moment, all she yearned for was to turn back the clock to a time when her life was uncomplicated. How had she managed to become entangled in this intricate web of despair? Sitting down for breakfast together, she tried to maintain a sense of normalcy for the sake of the boys.

Becks managed to do three loads of laundry and prepare lunch, making it seem like just another Saturday. However, all Becks could do was constantly check the time, feeling the weight of the day's events. At 4 pm all four of them got into Connor's car and dropped the boys at the football club.

"Daddy will pick you up at half past six," Connor said, as they waved their boys goodbye. Becks felt a surge of emotions, causing two tears to run down her cheeks. Swiftly, she brushed them away and wiped her nose.

"Are you OK? I know you can do this," Connor said.

"No, no I'm not OK but, tell me, what other choice do I have?" Becks asked. Silence was Connor's only response. He understood that any words he could offer would be futile in easing her burden.

Quietly they headed towards the old house, where Connor had skilfully parked Kerry's car away from prying eyes. Connor ran through the back gate, removed the safety chain from the front door, and hurried back to join Becks who had just stepped out of the vehicle. It was crucial to create the impression that Kerry was present. Stepping towards the entrance, a familiar voice echoed from the opposite side of the street.

"Hello, strangers, nice to see you back," Nigel, their neighbour, said.

"Hi, Nigel, lovely to see you," Becks said, as Connor waved, both displaying big smiles.

"What brings you back?" Nigel asked.

"The tenant is moving out today, we're just here to get the keys and inspect," Connor replied.

"Oh, right, never really saw much of her anyway, very quiet lady. I'll be sure to wave her off as she goes by," Nigel said. Becks took a deep breath before flashing a grin.

Together, they made their way to the entrance, where Becks discreetly shielded Connor as he inserted the key into the lock before Becks pressed the doorbell. As the door opened, Connor let out a loud voice.

"Hello, Kerry," he shouted as he went through the front door.

"What are you doing?" Becks asked quietly.

"Making it look realistic," Connor replied.

Becks then entered the downstairs washroom and swapped her attire for something she wouldn't wear even if her life depended on it. Skin-tight black leggings, a cropped jumper, a baseball cap, oversized sunglasses, trainer socks, and black trainers. With her makeup bag in hand, she meticulously layered on foundation, eyeshadow, and mascara before plumping up her lips. However, upon gazing at her reflection in the mirror, she was filled with disgust. After a deep breath, she walked out into the hallway.

"Wow, you look—" Connor started to say.

"If you say gorgeous, I will seriously take all of this off and slap you," she interrupted.

"No, you look like her, almost too much," he said.

"It isn't hard, half of the women out there look like this, nothing real about them," she said, with hatred in her voice.

Connor handed her a pair of sleek black leather gloves, then proceeded to pass her the driving licence and bank details, and hand over Kerry's phone. Becks placed the items, along with a pair of scissors, into a small shoulder bag. With utmost care, he shared the passcode and provided clear instructions on how to access the email account.

"You can do this. Be flirty, sexy, and, most of all, be confident. Look at her signature and copy it," he said calmly. While Becks was getting ready, Connor had already shifted his car, anticipating Becks' need for a speedy departure. Exiting the kitchen, she made her way to the back garden, circling to Kerry's car. Putting on her gloves, she opened the driver's side door, started the engine, and left the estate. Driving by Connor, she waved before turning to Nigel, ensuring he didn't catch a direct glimpse of her face.

"Becks and I are just going to clear up a little, we'll see you soon, Nigel," Connor shouted across the street.

"Best of luck with the new tenant," Nigel said.

"Thank you," he said, as he smiled and turned back around.

"Where do you want to start, love?" Connor shouted, to make it appear that Becks was still in the house.

Becks cautiously navigated the nine-mile journey, ensuring she remained inconspicuous. She parked the vehicle near the mobile cabin, still wearing her gloves. As she entered, cap and glasses on, her appearance drew the immediate attention of the men present.

"Kerry Reed, is it?" the man asked.

"Yes, good evening," Becks replied, with a flirtatious smile.

"Great, I'm Andy. Can I have your keys to check the vehicle over?" he asked. With her leather gloves still on, she passed him the key.

"Here you go," she said. Andy smiled, as he received the keys in his right hand.

"My colleague, Wayne, here, will go through the paperwork with you," he said. Taking a seat, Becks positioned herself on the edge of the chair, elegantly crossing her legs and maintaining a lowered gaze, making a conscious effort to suppress any involuntary movements or trembling.

"So we've had the email confirmation from your husband. You have the V5 and the copy of his passport, as well as your licence, is that right?" he asked.

"Yes, I do. I'm sorry, I must look so silly in these glasses. I suffer terribly from migraines and these just help me, you don't mind, do you?" she asked.

"Not to worry, I can see it's you," he replied, which helped her to relax slightly.

Andy returned after inspecting the vehicle and announced,

"OK, Mrs Reed, you have a few scuffs, so this is the best price I can give you." He tilted the iPad screen towards her.

"That's fine, I knew there were some areas of damage," she replied.

"If you could sign here, we'll get you on your way," Wayne said, placing the iPad in front of her. Becks removed her right glove and squiggled on the screen.

"Signatures never look right on these things, do they?" Becks said laughing.

"They never do," Wayne replied.

"Do you think you could book me a taxi, please, to Tree Hill?" Becks asked.

"Yes, sure. They're usually quick around here, the taxi rank is just over there," Wayne replied.

"Oh, I can walk over there," Becks said.

"No, it's OK, we have a system with them, they'll be over in a couple of minutes. The money should be in your account within four working days. It's been a pleasure, Mrs Reed, thank you," Andy said. As he opened the door for her, she smiled and exited the mobile hut with her hat, glasses and gloves still on. Without delay, the taxi came to a stop right in front of her.

"Taxi for Mrs Reed?" the taxi driver asked.

"Goodness, that was quick! Yes, thank you," Becks said, as she opened the back door of the taxi and sat in the back seat. Patiently, she waited in the car as the driver navigated through the congested streets.

Removing her glove, she retrieved her phone from her pocket and dialled Connor's number.

"It's done, see you at the house," she said down the phone quietly. The taxi driver pulled onto the estate, "You can drop me here on the left, thank you, keep the change," Becks said, passing him a twenty-pound note. As she took the money out of her bag, she dropped a hair bobble beside the seat in the process.

"Thank you, Mrs Reed," the taxi driver replied.

With her gloves still on, she exited the car and waited for the taxi to drive off before taking off her glasses and baseball cap and stashing them in a small shoulder bag along with the documents. She then let her hair loose and started walking quickly down the hill. As she walked, she used her earring to pop open the sim card slot on Kerry's phone, removed the sim card, sliced it in two with the scissors she'd stashed in her bag, and disposed of it in a nearby public bin.

Quickly, she sprinted towards the house at top speed. Turning the corner onto the street, she was grateful to find it deserted, feeling a wave of relief wash over her. She rushed to the back of the house, into the garden and in through the open back door. After shutting the door, she paused, feeling her heart pounding and her breath coming in short gasps before leaning her head back against the door. Gathering her strength, she stood tall and collected, making her way towards the downstairs bathroom where her clothes waited. With haste, she swiftly undressed out of Kerry's clothes and stuffed them into a bag, grabbing a wipe to cleanse away the caked-on makeup. Relief washed over her as she finally recognised her reflection in the mirror, both in appearance and in how she felt.

Connor and the boys arrived shortly after. With a quick stride, Connor hopped out of his vehicle and made his way towards the entrance. As he inserted his key into the lock, Becks was taken aback by the sudden noise.

Stepping inside, he found Becks looking just like her usual self and asked in a concerned manner "Are you OK?"

"Yes, I think so," Becks replied.

"You've done well, thank you," Connor replied. His smile lit up his face as he looked at his beautiful wife.

"Let's get out of here. These are her clothes," Becks replied, handing Connor the carrier bag.

Together, they made their way to the car, creating the illusion that she'd never left. As she settled into the passenger seat, she let out a long exhale.

She turned around and said, "Hi, boys, did you have fun at football?" while nervously taking a long sip of water. Her mouth felt as dry as a desert, leaving her parched and in need of hydration.

"Yes, we did. Are we moving back to this house Mummy?" Logan asked.

"No, sweetheart, Mummy was just doing some cleaning," Becks replied. As they drove past the house, Nigel came out of his front door and waved at them. Connor stopped and let the window of the driver's side down.

"See you again soon, Nigel," Connor said.

"Yes, it was lovely to see you all again. Did you get everything sorted?" Nigel asked.

"You'll have to ask the cleaning expert, I went to pick the boys up from football while Becks cleaned up," Connor replied.

"It wasn't too bad at all. Thankfully, she'd left the house in a clean condition, but we'll be back tomorrow to finish off," Becks answered, smiling.

"Great, best of luck, take care," Nigel replied. Grinning, Connor and Becks moved forward, leaving the cul-de-sac behind them.

Upon reaching their house, Becks took the lead and entered first, with the others following closely behind.

"Sort them out please, I need a shower," Becks said, as she walked up the stairs and shed her clothes before entering the soothing stream of water in the shower. After washing her hair, she stood and used soap to wash every part of her body.

She stepped out of the shower, wrapped a fresh towel across her chest and put on some baggy clothes. With her wet hair loose, she proceeded to gather the laundry from the basket and started the washing machine. Downstairs, she discovered that Connor had taken charge of dinner and had prepared pizza and salad. The boys were already seated at the table as if it were an ordinary Saturday night.

"I went to get the new slabs on my way to football. They're being delivered tomorrow morning at 8:30 am, I'll go and lay them first thing," he said to Becks calmly.

"Great, it will look lovely once it's done," she replied, as if in a daze.

As the evening meal concluded, Becks lovingly washed and tucked the boys into bed. After they drifted off to dreamland, she quietly entered their dimly lit rooms, perching herself on the edge of their beds. Gazing at their peaceful faces, a wave of sorrow washed over her. Unable to escape the ache in her heart, she kissed both their heads and left quietly.

As she climbed into bed, she left Connor downstairs alone. Sitting up, with the TV on mute and gazing into space, she appeared robotic, devoid of any emotion or sensation. Connor eventually made his way to the bedroom where she lay.

"I've tidied up the kitchen. Are you OK? Thank you, Becks, I couldn't have done this without you. Please, know how sorry I am and how grateful I am to you," Connor said.

"Yes, I know you are," she replied with half a smile, her eyes still unable to look at him.

"I take it everything went OK at the car place?" he asked.

"Yes. I think I put on a good act, not hard to act like a brainless bimbo," she answered.

"That must've been hard, I'm sorry I put you through that," he replied in sorrow.

"Yes, well, what other choice did I have? Let's go back and sort the house out tomorrow. The skip is arriving on Monday morning so at least we can sort out what to keep and what to get rid of. I've asked the childminder to take the boys out so we can get everything in order. I can then ring the estate agents on Monday and tell them that she's moved out," she said.

"Thank you, sounds like a good plan. I hope this is the end of it," he said.

"Me, too! Goodnight," she replied coldly.

"Goodnight, I love you," he said. As he looked at her, he stood up, bowed his head, and closed the bedroom door.

The following day, Connor was already awake and out of the house by 8 am. Becks, on the other hand, woke up at 8:20 am to find a note from him saying that he'd gone to the house and that the boys had already had breakfast. She called out the boys' names, prompting them to rush upstairs. With a smile on her face, she opened her arms wide as they jumped onto the bed. Nestled between her two precious children, she held them close, seeking comfort from the overwhelming anguish that consumed her.

"Have you had breakfast?" she asked.

"Yes, Daddy made us eggs and soldiers," Logan replied.

"That's great, so yummy. So, you guys are going to have a fun day, you're going out with Debbie. She's going to take you to the park, then out for lunch, and then swimming, while Mummy and Daddy get the old house cleaned. Then we'll have a nice dinner together later, OK?" Becks said.

"Yes, we love Debbie," Rory said.

"Good boys. Go and get washed and dressed, she'll be here soon," Becks said. Becks stepped into the shower, determined to freshen up and put her best foot forward. However, as she glanced at her reflection, she couldn't help but notice the growing shadows beneath her eyes. Undeterred, she swiftly gathered the boys' swim kits and brushed their hair.

After Debbie had collected the boys, she gathered cleaning supplies and loaded them into a bag. She then drove to the house and parked her car behind Connor's. As she stepped out, the sound of a radio playing music in the back garden reached her ears. Curious, she walked around the side of the house and witnessed Connor, wearing a white vest, casually laying slabs on top of where Kerry's body was. He seemed completely carefree, whistling away. She stood there, staring at him with a cold, piercing gaze.

"Hey, I didn't see you there. Are the boys OK?" he asked, smiling.

"Yes, the boys are fine. You've just moved on, haven't you?" she asked, with a confused look on her face.

"What do you mean?" he said quietly, as he came towards her.

"You, this, do you have any idea how messed up this scene is? Do you feel any remorse?" Becks asked in a quiet voice.

"I'm just trying to move forward. What's done, is done, and we have to move on. I'm sorry, I just wanted the neighbours to hear normality," he said.

"Yes, right, normality, of course!" she replied. Without blinking, she looked away from him and stared at the patio. "You've done a good job," she continued, walking into the house through the back door with her arms folded.

Connor felt embarrassed and at a loss for words when faced with Becks' constant barrage of negativity towards him. Every attempt to speak or act seemed to invite more criticism from her. The thought of finding a way to make it up to her seemed impossible to him.

Becks embarked on a thorough cleaning mission, tackling each room with determination. Fortunately, they had left behind most of their furniture, sparing Kerry from having any personal belongings in the house. The only item that she'd brought was the unsightly glass coffee table, which was now six feet under the ground along with its owner. Beginning in the living room, she tidied up the sofas, freshened the curtains, and spread carpet freshener around, making the space feel like home once more. Moving on to the kitchen, she emptied the fridge, freezer, and cupboards, boxing up all the dishes, utensils, and glasses, leaving the cupboards bare in no time.

She meticulously scrubbed the insides of every cupboard, ensuring no speck of dirt remained. The washing machine received a thorough cleansing as well, leaving it sparkling and fresh. As she pressed the button to start the dishwasher's cleaning cycle, she couldn't help but feel a pang of guilt at the amount of food wasted as she carried bin bags out to the bins. However, she quickly shifted her focus and diligently mopped the floor, restoring the kitchen to its pristine state in no time.

Heading upstairs, she'd already cleared out the majority of the drawers on the Friday. While in the master en suite, she suddenly heard the front door slam against the fastened chain, accompanied by a girl's loud shout.

"MUM! Every bloody time!" Suddenly, the front door slammed shut and the doorbell rang, causing her to abruptly halt. She then proceeded to knock on the back window, catching a glimpse of Connor hard at work.

"There's someone at the door," Becks whispered, pointing.

"Come down," Connor mimed back as he signalled with his hand. Connor entered the kitchen, threw on his t-shirt, and found Becks waiting at the foot of the stairs.

"Be calm, stick to the story," he signed to Becks with his hands. The door was now slightly ajar, resting on the safety chain. "Just a sec," Connor said. After shutting the door, Connor removed the chain and reopened it to find a well-dressed man with dark hair and, wearing a checked shirt tucked into jeans, accompanied by a young girl standing beside him.

"Hi, who are you? Where's Kerry?" the man asked, baffled by the two strangers standing in his ex-wife's house.

With a backpack slung over her shoulder, the girl exuded a carefree vibe. Her flowing light brown locks cascaded down her back, perfectly complementing her trendy bell-bottom jeans and stylish crop top.

"Hi, my name's Connor and this is my wife, Rebecca. We own this house. I'm sorry, who are you?" he asked.

"Michael Reed, Kerry's husband, and this is Darcy, our daughter. Where's Kerry?" he asked again.

"I don't know, she messaged us on Friday saying that she was moving out. We met her here yesterday afternoon and she gave us the keys back. Her belongings were packed and she drove off. Has she not told you?" Connor replied.

"What? She wouldn't do that, not so suddenly anyway," Michael replied.

"She's done it again hasn't she? Let me guess, she didn't pay you?" Darcy asked.

"I don't wish to disclose what happened, she sent my wife a message asking us to meet her here last night, she gave us the keys and left. I don't know any more, I'm sorry," Connor replied shyly.

"What about all my stuff?" Darcy asked.

"The rooms upstairs are practically empty, just the furniture that we left, I'm guessing she took most things with her. We're just packing up the last remaining bits, do you want to see it?" Becks asked.

"I need to see my room," Darcy shouted, as she barged past Becks and ran up the stairs. "I don't believe this!" Darcy shouted. Becks followed her upstairs; she caught sight of a fragile young girl in distress.

"She's so selfish, doing this to me again. I'm so sick of her," Darcy said.

"Doing what again, sweetheart?" Becks asked.

"This is what she does, she goes around, house-to-house, lives there for about six months, doesn't pay the rent and then moves on. Each time she's done this she's left me behind and it's always on a weekend when I'm with my dad. Then, she calls me about a month later saying sorry, and gets me to go back, it's just typical of her," Darcy said.

"I'm so sorry, Darcy, that really is sad," Becks said.

"Yeah, well, this time, if she thinks I'm bothering with her, she can think again, and that's all my stuff gone again, too. She can rot in hell for all I care!" Darcy ranted.

"I'm sure she's taken your belongings with her Darcy," Becks said in an attempt to console this broken little girl.

Darcy led the way down the stairs, with Becks close behind. Becks struggled to conceal the overwhelming emotions of guilt and sorrow that were etched across her face.

"She's done it again, Dad, let's just go. God, I hate her!" Darcy stated, as she stormed back to the car.

"I'm sorry. I'm guessing she left you out of pocket?" Michael asked.

"It's fine, we have the house back, that's all that's needed. Please, don't worry, focus on your daughter," Connor said, as Becks walked up behind him and gripped his upper arm.

"Appreciated, thank you. If you do get a forwarding address, or if she's left anything, please give me a call," Michael replied, handing Connor his business card.

"Yes, of course," Connor replied, reaching out to receive the card.

As Michael made his way back to his sleek black BMW, he smoothly accelerated and left the house behind. Meanwhile, Connor securely closed the door, reattached the chain, and let out a long, calming breath.

"Bloody hell!" he said, as he exhaled.

"I can't do this. She's lost her mum, she was heartbroken," Becks said sadly.

"Hey, hey, you heard her, she does this all the time, this is a good thing for us," Connor said, as he held Becks' shoulders. Becks jolted and removed his hands from her shoulders.

"Good for us? Good? None of this is good. You're so cool, lie after lie just pouring off your tongue. I don't feel that I even know you anymore," Becks shouted and pushed him away.

"Becks, please, be quiet, people will hear you," he said.

"This is torture, absolute torture," she said. With a determined stride, Becks made her way back upstairs, stamping her feet on every step.

Connor found himself at the foot of the staircase, unable to utter a word as his wife stormed away in anger. He knew he had no other option but to remain silent, she was correct in calling him a dishonest person. He returned outside to resume laying the slabs, while Becks scrubbed the bathrooms to remove any remnants of the past, and revitalised the curtains and carpets. As she surveyed the rooms, it felt as though Kerry's presence had been completely erased.

Becks wrapped up the cleaning session with the upstairs looking immaculate. She came downstairs to find Connor finishing the placement of the final few slabs, his music silent and a solemn expression on his face. With his hair cascading over his eyebrows, she observed him closely, recognising that he wasn't inherently bad, but rather a foolish man who'd succumbed to errors, much like she'd been manipulated by that wicked woman.

He looked up at her, "Are you OK?" Connor asked.

"Yes, I'm fine, the upstairs is finished," Becks said with a shy smile. Repeatedly, she lugged the bags of rubbish outside, making multiple trips through the back door, shoving them into the wheelie bin, and pressing her weight on the bags to push the rubbish down.

"The bins are due to be collected tomorrow, so at least it will all be gone," Becks said, as she walked past him.

"Good," Connor replied with a smile. As he lay the last slab into its place, Becks approached him.

"Here, you must be thirsty," Becks said, handing Connor a bottle of water.

"Thanks. I'm sorry, please, you have to know how sorry I am," Connor repeated, as he took a sip of water.

"Yes, I know you are," Becks replied.

Her gaze lingered on the immaculate patio he'd expertly constructed, her thoughts burdened, her heart shattered. Becks averted her gaze from him, her mind blank on what else to say. It was as if they were total strangers, their interactions filled with an awkwardness that couldn't be ignored.

Back inside the house, she carefully examined every room, ensuring there were no traces left of Kerry's presence. It was as if she'd never lived there at all. However, this time, an eerie chill hung in the air. The house had lost all traces of the joy they once shared. It now stood as a haunting reminder of the past two days that had turned all the beautiful memories sour.

"Inside is all clear and I've moved the things that need to go into the skip to the garage. I'm guessing we're coming back tomorrow?" Becks asked.

"I've taken tomorrow off work. I'll come first thing, touch up the paintwork, wait for the skip and fill it. I'll ask them to come straight back and collect it so it's not sitting on the drive," Connor replied.

"I need to go and get the boys. We need to give them some time, I feel like we've completely neglected them this weekend," Becks said.

"Yes, I know, we will. How about a takeaway tonight, they love a takeaway," Connor replied.

"Yes, that would be nice for them, thank you," Becks replied.

Longing for reconciliation, she yearned for harmony to be restored between them. The demise of their love left her questioning what had gone awry. Her affection for her husband and their small family remained unwavering, cherishing the bond of marriage. All she craved was the return of normalcy, a chance to mend their relationship.

"I'll go, see you back at home. Could you give the house a look over and make sure I've not missed anything, please?" Becks asked.

"Yes, of course I will. I'll just tidy up here, then I'll go and get the takeaway. Chinese OK?" Connor replied.

"Yes, please. See you soon," Becks said, as she turned and walked away.

As Becks made her way to her car, she settled into the driver's seat and inhaled deeply before stealing a glance at the house through her rearview mirror, pressing the accelerator and driving off. Connor tidied up the garden, cast his eye over every room, secured all the doors, reattached the chain on the front door as a precaution, and exited through the back door. He got into his car and drove away from the concealed crime scene. After travelling three miles, Connor stopped at a public bin, destroyed the erased phone by smashing the screen, and disposed of it.

As soon as Becks stepped into her house, she made up her mind to freshen up with a quick shower before the boys arrived. Shedding her soiled garments, she positioned herself beneath the water and let her mind wander back to the events of the past two days. After stepping out of the shower, Becks slipped into cosy jogging bottoms and a snug hoody. Suddenly, the doorbell chimed, announcing the arrival of Debbie and her boys, who had just returned from their day full of adventure. With excitement, Becks swung open the door and embraced her sons tightly, cherishing the warmth of their presence.

"Hi, have you had a nice day?" Becks asked, smiling.

"It was the best day," Rory answered.

"Great. Boys, straight upstairs please. Logan, can you run the bath? Daddy is bringing a takeaway home," Becks shouted up the stairs lovingly, as her boys ran off.

"Thank you, Debbie, we've managed to get a lot sorted today," Becks said.

"They've been wonderful, as always," Debbie replied. Becks fetched her purse from the side unit in the hallway and handed Debbie sixty pounds.

"Here you go, thank you again," Becks said.

"Anytime. Take care, bye," Debbie said, as she exited the front door.

After Becks had bathed the boys and dressed them in their pyjamas, Connor walked through the door, carrying a bag of food.

"Daddy!" Logan shouted with excitement.

"Here you go. I'll just have a quick shower," Connor said, handing Becks the large bag of food.

"OK, I'll get this plated up," Becks replied. In a flash, Connor dashed up the stairs, shedding his clothes and cleansing his body from the grime and perspiration. He wore fresh joggers and a t-shirt, then descended to join his family at the table.

The table was surrounded by their little family of four enjoying Chinese cuisine, with the boys playfully bantering and slurping noodles. Becks sat quietly, poking at her food, feeling the love for her little family that was now fractured. As she pondered over the events of the past two days, it seemed surreal, almost like a twisted nightmare.

Once dinner was done, she tucked the boys into bed and suddenly heard a crackling sound emanating from the backyard. Curiosity piqued, she peered out of the bedroom window at the back garden, only to discover Connor standing near the fire pit, beer in hand, tossing various objects into the flames. Becks decided to join him, stepping out into the cool night air.

"What are you doing?" Becks asked, as she wrapped a large shawl around herself, while balancing a hot cup of tea.

"Just getting rid of the last little bits. We need to burn our clothes, her clothes, her documents, we need to make sure there's nothing left tying us to her," Connor said.

"Yes, I just can't get over how calm you are," Becks said, as she placed both hands around the warm mug.

"Not on the inside. I'm terrified, guilty, sorry, angry at myself but so, so thankful to you," he replied, as he looked at her in the light of the fire.

"It would have been nice sitting around this warm fire. We loved this in the last house, didn't we?" Becks asked.

"Yes, we did. I never thought I would be burning a dead woman's clothes in it though," Connor said as he exhaled.

"Yes, this has been an absolute nightmare from start to finish. This woman has manipulated us, she's ruined what we had," Becks said with regret.

"She hasn't ruined us, nothing can ruin us, so long as we have each other, that's all we need. Well, it's all I need anyway,"

Connor said with sincerity, while he poked the fire with a wooden stick.

"But it wasn't, otherwise you wouldn't have acted in that way," Becks said, as she hung her head, turned her back, and walked inside.

Inside, she began organising her work items, and prepared her outfit for the next day before settling into bed for the night. Half an hour later, Connor walked into the bedroom. Becks was lying in bed, laptop open, papers spread around her.

"All sorted?" Becks asked.

"Yes. I've made sure there's no residue left. I've left a log on there to let it smoulder for an hour. I'll go and put it out in a little while," he replied.

"OK, great," Becks said, as she continued to read.

"Becks?" Connor asked, as he started to walk towards her.

"Please, don't. I don't want another row, and I'm certainly not ready for you to come anywhere near me, so please, respect me enough to give me some time, please," Becks replied.

"Yes, of course, I respect you more than anyone in this world, please know that," Connor said, and walked out of the room.

Becks inhaled deeply, trying to regain her focus as she scrolled through her emails. However, her mind was elsewhere, so she closed her eyes and rested her head against the headboard. Meanwhile, Connor returned outside and settled beside the fading fire pit, sipping on his second beer while gazing up at the twinkling night sky. Overwhelmed with guilt, he wondered if she would ever find it in her heart to forgive him. And more importantly, would he ever be able to forgive himself? After twenty minutes, he extinguished the fire by pouring water over it, covered it with the lid, and made his way to the spare room for the night.

In the dead of night, Connor was abruptly jolted awake by a piercing scream that shattered the silence.

"Becks?" he cried out, as he raced down the hallway into their bedroom. Becks was sat up crying. He came towards her and held her. As she started to cry on his shoulder, she welcomed his embrace.

"I keep seeing her. Every time I close my eyes, I keep seeing her," Becks cried.

"It's OK, I'm here, I'm not going anywhere, I've got you," he said, as he pulled her closer. As he reclined, Becks nestled in the crook of his arm, breathing in the comforting scent she'd longed for. Lost in the moment, she drifted off to sleep, snuggled against him. He held her throughout the night, savouring the presence of his beloved wife in his embrace once more.

At 6 am, Becks' alarm started to chime. She'd fallen into a deep sleep, feeling as though she'd been hit over the head with a frying pan. She sat up suddenly, noticing a sleepy Connor beside her in the bed.

"Morning," he said, smiling with his mouth closed. She was startled.

"Morning, I better get up," she said strongly. Quickly, she sprang out of bed, overwhelmed with shame for succumbing to her weakness. A sense of unease hung in the air, creating an uncomfortable distance between them, almost as if they were strangers.

"Yes, I'll go and start getting the boys sorted," he replied.

"That would be helpful, thank you," Becks said awkwardly.

As the morning sun streamed through the windows, Connor walked down the stairs with a spring in his step. He switched on the coffee machine, filling the air with the rich aroma of freshly brewed coffee. With a culinary flair, he began preparing a delightful breakfast feast of eggs, bacon, toast, and fluffy pancakes. Afterwards, he gently roused his two boys from their beds, planting tender kisses on their sleepy heads and filling their hearts with warmth and love.

"Good morning, boys, it's a beautiful day, and it's breakfast time. Daddy has cooked breakfast for you," Connor said. Coming down the stairs dragging their drowsy bodies, their faces brightened at the sight of the vast array of food spread out before them.

"Why are we having this on a Monday?" Rory asked.

"First day back. It's always good to start the first day with a big breakfast," Connor replied, smiling.

Becks walked down the stairs in her elegant trouser suit, only to be met with the infectious laughter and playful banter coming from Connor.

"What's all this?" she asked, as she kissed the boys and rubbed her fingers through their hair.

"Daddy's made breakfast," Logan said.

"Wow, that's great," Becks replied.

"Here, have a seat," Connor said, pulling a chair out for Becks to sit down.

"No, I'm fine with a slice of toast and a cup of coffee. Thank you, though. Boys, go upstairs and get dressed, we need to leave early this morning," she replied.

"Becks," Connor said.

"Not now, please, I can't be late today. And I'm sorry about last night, it won't happen again," Becks said. Overwhelmed by a mix of embarrassment and vulnerability, she found herself exposed. She was angry with herself for desperately relying on him. However, deep within her, a burning desire to regain her strength ignited, urging her to strive for independence and resilience.

"You don't need to be sorry, I loved it, I loved lying with you again," Connor replied lovingly. Becks locked eyes with him, but quickly averted her gaze and retreated upstairs, leaving Connor standing alone in the kitchen, a towel casually hanging over his shoulder.

While Becks assisted the boys with their hair and final preparations, she eventually made her way back downstairs.

"So, you'll sort the skip out today?" Becks asked.

"Yes, I'll make sure everything is clean. Will you ring the estate agent?" Connor asked.

"Yes, I'll ring them after 9 am, and ask them if they're free today to come and meet you there," Becks replied.

"Yeah, that would be great, if they can," Connor replied.

"OK, bye. Boys, say bye to Daddy," Becks said.

"Bye guys," Connor said, as he waved his hand and closed the front door behind them.

Connor faced his deserted home once again, the overwhelming quietness piercing through him. He tidied the kitchen before heading upstairs for a shower. After the events of the previous night, he couldn't help but feel a sense of optimism. He sensed a glimmer of hope and thought that maybe Becks was beginning to forgive him, filling him with profound happiness.

Becks arrived at school, escorted the boys to breakfast club, and entered her office feeling calm. She assumed her role as head teacher, exuding professionalism as she led the morning assembly with confidence and grace.

Meanwhile, after taking a quick shower, Connor headed back to the house. Just as he arrived, the skip delivery truck pulled up right behind him.

"Morning, great timing. Thank you, just there on the drive," Connor said.

"OK, mate, just give us a call when you're ready for it to be collected," the delivery driver said.

"It'll be ready in about an hour, mate, can you get back today?" Connor asked.

"Yeah, I have three more deliveries this morning, I can be back by lunchtime?" the driver asked.

"Yes, that would be perfect, thanks, I'll pay you then," Connor replied. As he made his way through the back gate whistling a tune, he couldn't help but pause and admire his handy work on the newly constructed patio. Filled with a sense of accomplishment, he took a moment to inhale deeply before heading towards the garage. Once inside, he began clearing out the remaining broken slabs, discarded bin bags, and fragments of furniture. In no time, the skip was filled to the brim, and the house regained its fresh and revitalised appearance.

Becks discussed with the estate agent and it turned out that they were already conducting a visit on the estate. Tony, the agent, arrived at the house at 11:15 am and as Connor opened the door, a sigh of relief escaped. A feeling of harmony washed over him as he witnessed everything falling seamlessly into place.

"Good morning, I'm Tony, nice to meet you, you must be Connor?" he asked, with his towering height and slender frame. Tony displayed an air of professionalism in his black suit, crisp white shirt, and vibrant red tie. His professional appearance was complemented by his neatly groomed short hair and distinguished grey beard. As he extended his hand towards Connor, he confidently introduced himself.

"Yes, good morning, thank you for coming so soon," Connor replied.

"I was doing a viewing at 10:30 am down the road, so it made sense and, of course, I need to hear what's happened. Such a sudden change of heart, your wife explained?" Tony asked in his Geordie accent.

"Yes, it was a shock to us too, a text out of nowhere, and she just left. She was all packed up and ready to go when we arrived here on Saturday, so, yes, we're very grateful and happy that it's over," Connor said.

"It's always a good day when a bad tenant leaves and the house is yours again, and it looks like you've been very busy over the weekend?" Tony asked.

"Yeah, we both work during the week, so we just got cracking to get it sorted," Connor explained.

"Well, it looks great. Your wife said you would like us to rent it out for you and fully manage it?" Tony asked.

"Yes, I think that will be best. We just need to have a good tenant in next and forget this ever happened," Connor continued.

"Well, I have my camera in the car, I'll get some pictures, and post it online by the end of today for you," Tony said.

"Perfect, thank you. I'm just going to mow the lawn, then you can include the garden in your pictures," Connor said.

Tony explored each room, snapping photos as he marvelled at the beauty of the house. Connor retrieved his neglected lawn mower from the garage, that he'd left behind for the tenant to use, and began mowing the overgrown grass. Walking up and down the garden he avoided stepping onto the patio, feeling a chill run down his back each time he passed by.

Tony walked out of the back door.

"Mr Jones, inside is done, it's very clean, it looks great. Oh, and have you put down a new patio?" Tony said, as he walked towards it and went to stand on the slabs.

"Don't stand on them yet, they might not be dry!" Connor shouted.

"Oh, yes, so sorry, don't want to undo your hard work," Tony replied, as he jerked his body sideways.

"The old slabs were broken, uneven and unsafe to be honest, so I just did it over the weekend. Luckily, it's only a small patio," Connor said, as he laughed nervously.

"You've done a good job," Tony said.

After Connor had finished cutting the grass, Tony took his last photos and then departed, leaving Connor behind to wait for the skip to be collected. Returning inside with a container of white paint, he touched up any spots that required attention. While down on his hands and knees, painting the skirting board, the doorbell chimed. He stood up and watched as the skip was hauled off the ground. He retrieved cash from his wallet and felt a sense of relief to bid farewell to the last of Kerry's belongings.

"Hi again, neighbour," said a familiar voice from across the road.

"Oh, hi, Nigel, how are you?" Connor asked.

"Good, thank you. All empty?" Nigel asked.

"Yes, all empty, ready for the next tenant now," Connor replied.

"Well, good luck with it. I hope the next one is a looker like the last one," Nigel said, winking.

"I bloody don't!" Connor muttered under his breath to himself, as he turned around and walked back to the house. Nigel, a former professional who had spent his younger years as a postman, possessed an insatiable curiosity and a knack for prying into everyone's affairs within the neighbourhood. Despite his slender physique and receding hairline, he had an uncanny ability to notice even the smallest of details.

Connor glanced at the house and, just as he pressed the handle on the door, a sleek white Audi pulled up and parked outside the house. The car's blaring music caught his attention, and he noticed two individuals inside. The man appeared tall and thin, giving off an impression of someone struggling with addiction. On the other hand, the woman behind the wheel was on the heavier side, in her late thirties, and had a rough appearance that the Brits might describe as 'dog rough'. Her arm was adorned with tattoos, her hair was streaked with pink, and she had numerous piercings.

"Shit, who's this now?" he said to himself, with a disappointed look on his face.

He removed his hand from the door handle and stood tall.

"Hi, can I help you?" Connor asked the pair, who were now making their way to the front door.

"Who are you?" the man asked.

"I own this house," Connor replied.

"We're here to see Kerry," the woman answered.

"She moved out," Connor replied.

"No, she wouldn't do that without telling us," the woman replied.

"I don't know what to tell you, she left on Saturday. She gave us the keys back and left," Connor repeated.

"Let me go in and check," the woman said, as she took out her keys.

"You have a key?" Connor asked.

"Yeah, of course," the woman answered.

"Well, I need that back, she's moved out," Connor repeated.

"She wouldn't just leave. I'm her best mate, she wouldn't go without telling me," the woman said with such repulsion, looking Connor up and down.

"I'm not going to repeat myself; she's gone. I'll take you inside to show you, but I'm telling you, she doesn't live here anymore," he said, as he walked back towards the door.

As he swung open the front door, they strolled in as if it were their own home, seamlessly blending in with the surroundings.

"Something isn't right, she wouldn't do this," the woman said.

"I don't know what to say to you. If you give me your name and number, I'll call you if I get a forwarding address," Connor replied.

"What's your name? Are you Connor?" she asked.

His heart skipped a beat. "Yes, Connor Jones," he said confidently, his head held high.

"Yeah, Connor, got it. Don't see it myself to be honest, but hey," she answered, smirking at him. Connor stood still and stared at her, making sure he didn't make a move.

"No stress babe, I just need to check something though," she said, as she barged past him and walked upstairs.

"What are you doing? You can't just barge in here," Connor said.

"I'm doing nothing, I just left something," she replied, as she rooted in the fitted wardrobe of the spare bedroom.

She stood at the top of the stairs holding a plastic bag.

"She left this, John, why would she leave this?" she said, as she flashed the bag.

"What's that?" Connor asked.

"None of your business. Did you kick her out, did you force her? I know all about you, I know everything," she said in a deep voice, as she came up close to him, chewing her gum with her mouth open.

"Please, leave now. Oh, and I need your key," he said, as he opened the front door and held out his hand.

"Whatever, here, have your key," she said, as she brushed past him. As he shut the door behind her, his breath quickened.

"No, please," he whispered urgently. His heart was pounding.

Racing up the stairs, he entered the spare bedroom only to discover the wardrobe door ajar. Inside, he noticed parcel tape, clearly used to secure something to the wall within the wardrobe. Acting in panic, he grabbed a chair and meticulously searched every nook and cranny, removing drawers from dressers and bedside tables. Finally, beneath the drawer of the master bedroom's bedside table, he found a USB stick firmly taped underneath. Panic surged through him.

"What the hell is this?" he said to himself. He stashed it away in his pocket, retrieved his phone, and navigated to Richard's contact. Tapping the dial button, the phone rang merely twice, filling him with immense gratitude as his friend's voice echoed through the receiver.

"Hello," said Richard.

"Hi, Rich, it's Connor. Listen, I need a favour, mate, our tenant has gone and I need the locks changing, soon. Any chance you can get here today?" Connor asked his friend, who just happened to be a locksmith.

"Yes, mate. I'm due to finish about 4:30 pm. At your old place, is it? Front and back? I'll pick up a couple of locks when I'm out later," Rich replied.

"You're a diamond, mate. Yes, both front and back locks, please, and thank you," Connor replied.

At 4 pm, Connor called Becks.

"Hi, how was your day?" Connor asked.

"It was fine, thank you. How was your day?" she replied.

"Eventful. I had two new visitors looking for Kerry, they'd stashed something in the spare bedroom wardrobe upstairs. Whatever it was, was inside a plastic bag and taped to the inner wall, wouldn't know it was there unless you searched for it," he said.

"Jesus! Are you serious?" Becks asked.

"Yeah, the woman took it, I didn't want to fight with her, she looked like she'd been dragged up from birth. I'm guessing drugs, absolute scum!" Connor answered, repulsed.

"I'm so sorry, I can't believe I fell for this woman's lies, she's just repulsive," Becks replied with dismay.

"You have nothing to be sorry for. We don't believe these people exist because we're good people who would never treat anyone this way. She was a good actress, I'll give her that, with her rich exterior. I'm just so sorry that it's unfolded like this," he said sincerely.

"I, I don't want this to be the end of us, I don't. I want our boys to grow up with two parents; to be good men. I want them to have the best," she said.

"Me too, sweetheart, me too. I'll do whatever it takes to make this right," he replied.

"Just be patient with me, I need time," Becks asked.

"Anything. I'll do anything to make this right, I'll make it up to you, I promise. I'll be a little longer, this woman who came today had a key, so Rich is coming over to change the front and back locks. I want to be safe, so I think it's best to change them," Connor said.

"Good idea, I'll have dinner ready when you come in, maybe we can sit and have dinner together?" she asked.

"I would love that, thank you," he said, with a smile on his face. After a long struggle, a sense of tranquillity washed over him, and his sole desire was to regain control of his life. It had been days since he'd experienced any comforting words from Becks, and he cherished every moment of it.

Richard made a punctual entrance at 5 pm, ensuring he was right on schedule. Richard, a towering and muscular individual, was well acquainted with exercise routines. Connor first encountered him at the gym, and they instantly formed a strong bond. Richard boasted an impressive upper body dominated by muscle mass, often sporting a t-shirt, hoodie, shorts, and work boots.

In just under an hour, he skilfully installed brand new locks on both the front and back doors, leaving the house secure and protected.

"New patio? Did you lay that?" Rich asked.

"Yes, the old one was uneven and unsafe, so I laid it yesterday," Connor replied.

"Looks good. You should've given me a shout, I could've come and helped you," Richard said.

"Thanks, it was quite easy, I enjoyed doing it," Connor replied.

"Don't be swapping your desk job to a manual job now, will you? No money in this, mate!" Richard said in jest. Connor smiled and stayed quiet. "Here, mate," Rich said, as he handed Connor the new keys.

"Thank you, this has been a nightmare. Here, please take this," Connor replied, as he handed him fifty pounds.

"Sounds it, pal. Put that money away, beers on you next time. Right, I better be off, we'll go for that beer next week, yeah?" Rich said, as he got in his van and drove off.

Connor fiddled with the keys in his hands, flashing a smile at his friend. Suddenly, a wave of reality washed over him, causing him to pause. He glanced down at the keys and pocketed them along with the USB stick, then locked the doors, and hopped into his car. As he pulled into the driveway of his home, he entered through the front door, greeted by a delightful aroma wafting through the air.

"Hi, I'm home," he said.

"Daddy, Daddy guess what, we played football and I scored two goals today," Rory said.

"Wow, that's great, well done," Connor replied, as he lifted him into his arms.

"Hi, dinner will be ready in a minute, I've made lasagne," Becks said.

"Great, I'm starving. Do I have time to quickly shower and change?" Connor asked.

"Yes, yes of course," Becks replied. Connor walked upstairs, entered his office, secured the USB stick in a drawer, and locked it.

He then proceeded to the bedroom, undressed and stood under the shower, lost in contemplation. Memories of Suzy's tragic fate haunted him, the push, the stake, her face when she realised, her body flopping, lifeless, the sound of her body hitting the ground when they threw her into the hole. The images flashed before his eyes, causing him to shake his head in disbelief before drying off and changing into comfortable clothing. He walked slowly down the stairs and a wave of rejuvenation washed over him. Taking his seat at the dinner table, surrounded by his loving wife and children, he relished in the simple joy of feeling normal once more. Unbeknownst to the boys, their parents concealed the heartache and stress they were enduring. Engaging in light conversation, Connor and Becks exchanged a tender glance, exchanging smiles that spoke volumes as they savoured their ordinary family meal.

Becks tucked the boys into bed, while Connor headed to his office. He settled into his chair, unlocked the drawer, and inserted the USB stick into his computer. Feeling overwhelmed, he opened the files to find numerous folders, one was labelled 'houses'. Clicking on it, he discovered various addresses, Clover Court, Regent Street, Victoria Avenue, Gulf Street, and Pear Court. Selecting Pear Court, their rented house address, he found another folder named, 'Connor 38'. Opening it, he found pictures of himself – the hotel images that he'd hoped to never see again – and a photo of his driving licence. There were pictures of Becks, the boys, and court paperwork. His rage intensified as he scrolled through images of his loved ones on the woman's device. Clicking on a folder labelled 'Clover Court', and a subfolder, 'Geoff 44', he discovered distressing photos of a man named Geoff in compromising positions, bound and clad in black leather. Moving on to Victoria Avenue, he found another folder, 'Alan 56', filled with similar images of men who had fallen victim to her schemes.

Folder upon folder, each labelled with names and accompanied by pictures. This woman was undoubtedly skilled, and Connor found himself ensnared in her web. Curiosity getting the better of him, he opened a file titled 'PDF bank statements' and discovered a staggering amount of money flowing in from various sources. Just on October's statement alone, she'd received a hefty eight thousand pounds. Overwhelmed and unsure of his next move, Connor was startled by the sudden entrance of Becks.

"What are you doing?" Becks asked.

"Nothing, just preparing some things for work tomorrow," Connor answered.

"Why are you lying to me?" Becks asked, as she stared at him straight in the eyes.

Exhaling deeply, Connor replied, "I found a USB stick in the house. It has pictures of men on it. She was doing this to a lot of people, zero standards by the looks of it, all middle-aged, balding men who, I'm guessing, had money." He felt utterly ashamed.

"Let me see," she said, as she walked towards him.

"I don't think you'll want to see," he replied.

"I want to see," Becks said sternly. Connor sat down and began to review the files containing the names of the men, while Becks' face twisted in disgust.

"In this folder, here," Connor said, as he clicked on the icon.

"And where are you?" she asked.

"Becks, please," Connor said desperately.

"I want to see," Becks demanded.

As Connor clicked on Pear Court, she was shocked to see her husband lying naked in a hotel bedroom, with his clothes scattered on the floor. She stared at the screen in disbelief, then glanced down to wipe some fluff off her trousers while clearing her throat.

"Right," she said, as she fidgeted with her fingers.

"I'm sorry," he said. He reached for her hand and Becks immediately pulled away.

"Can I ask you a question?" Becks asked.

"Yes, anything," he replied.

"Was she better than me? Was she better at sex?" she asked, like a naive school child.

"God, no! She was a mistake, she got inside my head. I'm not going to lie, I was flattered. I was flattered with the attention, but no way was she better than you. You're the love of my life, nothing and no one is better than you. I'm ashamed of myself for letting this woman do this to me, to us. I can't tell you how angry I am for being so weak, I could just punch myself," he said with emotion.

Becks looked at him square in the face, "But you said we were stale. Is it not fun with me anymore? Did she do things to you that I don't?" Becks asked, with a look of desperation on her face.

"No, I know I can ask anything of you and you'll do it. I can't explain it. I'm a man and a woman threw herself at me. I haven't had that before, it was stupid and selfish, I feel nothing but regret," Connor replied.

"Did you use protection?" Becks inquired.

Connor met her gaze with a heavy heart, "No, Becks, I did not." His face bore a sombre expression in response. She exhaled sharply, her eyes shut in a mix of astonishment and letdown.

"Seeing this, all those men she's been with, I want you to go and get tested. I can't be with you again until you've been screened. Jesus, we've had sex so many times since," Becks said in disbelief.

"Yes, yes, we have. I understand. I'll call tomorrow and book an appointment," he said, as he placed his hands on Becks' hands.

With his touch, she flinched and moved her hand away quickly.

"I need to go to bed. What are you going to do with that stick?" she asked.

"I'll erase it and get rid of it, she didn't have a laptop in the house. Well, I didn't see one, did you?" he asked.

"No, there wasn't one there, but why would she have a USB if she didn't have a computer?" Becks asked.

"I don't know. There's no guarantee that these images aren't somewhere else," he said nervously.

"God, I hope not," she replied, and walked out of the door. Suppressing her emotions, she made her way to their bedroom. Connor spent twenty minutes scouring through Kerry's documents, searching for anything valuable, but eventually gave up.

Realising the futility of his actions, and the risk of keeping the information, he deleted all traces of it from his computer, ensuring no evidence remained. He hoped to avoid any future repercussions from his actions. He stood up, walked out of his office and down the hallway towards Becks. He opened the door and there, in their marital bed, lay his beautiful wife.

"I just wanted to make sure you were OK?" Conor asked.

"Yes, I'm fine. I need to go to sleep," she replied bluntly.

"Yes, of course. I just wanted to make sure you were OK, that's all, goodnight," he said.

"Goodnight," she replied, as she leaned over and turned off her side lamp.

Lying in bed, she faced the bathroom, tears streaming down her face. Despite her efforts to wipe them away, they continued to fall. Unable to hold back any longer, she let out a muffled cry, her hand covering her mouth as she sobbed uncontrollably. Connor could hear her cries. Rising from bed to stand outside the bedroom door, he was torn between the desire to comfort her and the fear of rejection. He sat in the hallway, knees bent, elbows on knees, head against the wall, his hands covering his face, waiting for her sobs to subside. Despite their close physical proximity, their emotional distance seemed insurmountable. After half an hour, she finally succumbed to sleep, while he struggled to rise from the floor, his joints now stiff, and return to his bed. As he rested his head on the pillow, haunting images flooded his mind, fuelling a deep anger towards the deceased woman. At that moment, he found twisted satisfaction in her demise.

The following day started with the usual routine, with Becks and the boys heading to school and work. However, this time, Connor was there, being supportive and helpful to Becks as she got ready for school. Becks left with the boys, while Connor went to work, making it seem like just another typical Tuesday. It was his first day back at work since the incident, and he felt anxious about moving forward after taking someone's life.

As he eased back into the chaotic atmosphere of his bustling office, he couldn't shake off the nagging discomfort of having to call the sexual health clinic. During his lunch break, he shut his office door, searched for their contact number online, and reluctantly scheduled an appointment for the following morning at 10 am. Anxiety consumed him once more, fearing the possibility of contracting something. How would he break the news to Becks? By the time the day ended, he found himself drowning in an overwhelming workload, his short break only adding to the mounting pile of tasks.

By 5 pm, he was nowhere near finished with his tasks. He called Becks and she answered immediately.

"Hello," she answered.

"Hi, I'm so sorry, it's been a ridiculous day, and the work has just piled up with me not being here. Do you mind if I stay late and get this finished? I have that appointment at the clinic in the morning, so I won't be in first thing," Connor said.

"Yes, of course, if you need to stay then that's fine, the boys have football at six anyway. Will you eat there, or shall I get you something?" Becks asked.

"No, I'll eat here. I should be home for nine, is that OK?" Connor asked.

"You don't have to ask me, I'm not your keeper," Becks replied.

"I know. I just want you to be comfortable and I want you to know where I am," Connor said.

"Are you inside my mind now?" Becks asked in a sarcastic tone.

"I can hear it in your voice. I know it's going to take time for you to trust me again, but I've learnt from my mistake. I'll never do anything like that again, I promise," he replied.

"OK, I trust you," she said hastily. She put the phone down, and stood and stared into space for a minute while clutching her phone.

"Mummy!" Logan shouted, which brought Becks out of her daydream.

"Yes, sweetheart, sorry. Come on let's get you guys ready," she replied.

Connor was engrossed in his work while Becks hurried the boys into the car.

On their way to football practice, she decided to take a detour past Connor's office. As they drove by the car park, she noticed his car in the staff parking bay, alone. Looking up at his office window, she saw him sitting there with his glasses on, deeply focused on his computer. Feeling guilty for jumping to conclusions, her phone suddenly rang.

"Hello," she answered.

"Hey, did you just drive by here?" Connor asked.

"Yes, we did," she replied.

"Becks—" he started to talk, but she interrupted.

"Anyway, the boys are going to be late for football, see you when you get home, OK, bye." With a sense of urgency, she uttered the words and swiftly hung up the call.

Connor, feeling the weight of the situation, gently returned his phone to its place on the desk. He then took off his glasses, massaged his tired eyes, and thought, *Will she ever have faith in me again?*

At 9 pm, Connor arrived home to find the boys peacefully asleep in their beds. Becks was cosily lying in bed, engrossed in her laptop. He quietly made his way upstairs and stood by the bedroom door, taking in the scene before him.

"Hi, are you OK?" he asked.

"Yes, I'm fine. I have an important meeting tomorrow," she replied.

"Becks, I—" he started.

"Can we not, please? I'm tired. I'm tired of going over and over this. I shouldn't have driven by your office. I had a weak moment, it won't happen again," Becks said, interrupting him. "

Sure. I'm just going to have a shower, I'll try not to disturb you," he replied.

"Did you say your clinic appointment is tomorrow?" she asked.

"Yes, 10 am. I'll go to the office early in the morning, try and get a few bits done, then go," he replied. Without uttering another sound, her mind filled with a whirlwind of thoughts and words. She simply gazed down at her computer screen, attempting to focus as much as possible.

After another restless and destitute night of sleep, the following morning arrived. Connor, already awake and dressed, was ready to leave before anyone else. By the time the boys gathered for breakfast, he was already on his way out the door.

"Have a good day, I'll try and be back on time. Fish and chips tonight, boys?" Connor asked, which was well received by his over-excited children. By 7:30 am, Connor was already at the office, diving headfirst into his work. However, by 9:40 am, he found himself walking towards the clinic, feeling an overwhelming sense of embarrassment.

As a thirty-eight-year-old married man and a father of two, it was quite uncomfortable for him to be in such a situation. He reluctantly took a seat in the waiting room, filled out the necessary forms, and anxiously waited for his turn. The tables held a collection of outdated magazines, while the sterile surroundings of white walls added to his growing uneasiness.

"Connor Jones," the nurse shouted. Anxious, he rose to his feet, scanning the room to avoid any familiar faces, before striding confidently into the consultation room where the nurse greeted him with an introduction.

"Good morning, I'm Nicole. So, I'll take some history, we need to do a blood test and a swab, and then we'll go from there," she said cheerily.

"Great, thanks. How long will this take?" Connor asked.

"About thirty minutes," Nicole answered. Question after question poured out of her mouth, causing Connor's irritation to grow.

He'd always been composed, and his sexual experiences were almost non-existent before this encounter. After taking his blood samples, and an embarrassing swab, she reassured him that the results would arrive within forty-eight hours. She inquired about any other symptoms he might have experienced but, fortunately, he hadn't encountered any so far. Connor rose from his seat, expressing gratitude to the nurse, and swiftly exited the clinic, heading back to work. Along the way, he made a detour to the shop, purchasing cakes for his team as a peace offering for his recent erratic behaviour.

As Becks went about her usual school routine, she also had to attend a governor's meeting, a bittersweet experience that always brought mixed emotions. However, on this particular day, her mind was elsewhere. She felt a sense of loneliness, realising that she had no one. She kept her thoughts and feelings to herself, appearing reserved on the outside while silently screaming on the inside. At day's end, she gathered the boys, returned home, and at 5:30 pm, Connor arrived with fish and chips, as he'd pledged. Setting the table, they sat down once more, trying to maintain a facade of normalcy during dinner. However, it was far from normal. Barely a week had passed, yet on the exterior Connor seemed unaffected by the recent events. Despite his repeated apologies, his actions showed no remorse for the woman he'd killed, putting his entire family and their futures at risk.

Becks put the boys to bed and went downstairs where Connor was sat watching TV, the neck of the beer bottle nested between his fingers,

"How did your appointment go?" she asked.

"Fine. Embarrassing. Should get the test results back within forty-eight hours," he replied.

"OK, good," she answered.

"I'll never do anything like this ever again, please know this," he said, as he sat up and faced her.

"I certainly hope not. Oh, and I love how you chose that seat to sit on. I want that chair out of this house!" she replied in a disgusted manner, and turned bluntly and walked upstairs. His expression fell as he took another gulp from his beer. Abruptly standing up, he kicked the chair with his right foot.

Becks made her way to the bedroom, feeling a mix of emotions, emptiness, anger, frustration, sadness, and deep disappointment. Her mind urged her to forgive and be a family for the sake of their boys, but her heart was shattered, yearning to release a scream of anguish. They retreated to their separate beds once more, their hearts heavy with sorrow and burdened by remorse.

While Becks was working the next morning, she unexpectedly received a phone call from the estate agent while sitting at her desk.

"Hello," answered Becks.

"Good morning, Mrs Jones, it's Tony from Wise Move, is it OK to talk?" he asked.

"Good morning, yes, I can talk," she answered.

"We have a young family interested in your rental property, husband and wife with a daughter, and another one on the way.

They would like to view the property. Would you like me to show them around, or do you want to do it?" Tony asked.

"If you could, Tony, please. I want this fully managed now, I don't want any more, mishaps, if you like," Becks replied.

"Yes, of course. I'll go over later and show them around," Tony said.

"Oh, Connor had the locks changed, do you know if he's brought the new keys to you?" she asked.

"No, I don't believe so," Tony replied.

"No problem. I'll call him now and ask for him to drop them over to you at lunchtime," she replied.

Becks put the phone down and rang Connor immediately. With minimum warmth, she harshly uttered, "Hi, the estate agent has a couple interested in renting the house, have you given them the new keys?"

"No, I need to get more cut. I can go over at lunch, get a couple of sets cut and drop them in," Connor replied.

"Yes, if you can, thank you. I've asked them to fully manage this, I don't want anything to do with this from now on," Becks said.

"Yes, of course, just let them deal with it," he replied, in an attempt to support her.

"So, please, just think about who you sleep with in future," Becks said abruptly.

"Becks?" Connor asked.

"Sorry, I shouldn't have said that, but we don't want any repeats, do we?" Becks asked.

"I'll never, ever do anything like this again, you have to believe me," Connor begged.

"I don't have to do anything, just get the keys sorted, please," Becks said firmly.

After ending the call, Connor sighed and ran his hands through his hair. Around noon, he headed out to have a spare set of keys made, leaving two sets with the estate agent, and keeping the other for himself. As he made his way back to work, the sun cast its warm glow upon him. Taking a moment to rest, he found a spot in the precinct, and sat on a small wooden bench sipping on his bottle of water. Observing the bustling world around him, he couldn't help but wonder how his life had led him to this point. After a brief respite, he rose from his seat and strolled back to his office, ready to wrap up the rest of his afternoon. The feeling of complete letdown consumed his thoughts, making it impossible for him to break free from it.

That evening, after dinner, the kids had drifted off to sleep and Becks was lounging in bed with her laptop as usual, when Connor popped in to say hello.

"Did the estate agent ring you back?" Connor asked.

"No, I'm sure they will tomorrow," she answered.

"Listen, about what you said, please, you need to know that I've learnt from my mistake. That's what it was, a mistake," Connor said.

Becks was overcome with a profound feeling of irritation. She closed her laptop and said, "If all of this hadn't happened, if she wasn't our tenant and you hadn't killed her, would you even have told me?"

He paused for a moment. "Honest answer, I don't know," Connor replied, as he held his hands up.

"Because you were quite happy after you slept with her – twice, was it? To come to my parents, get into bed with me, without saying a word, without feeling any guilt," Becks replied.

"I felt so much guilt, my every being felt guilty to you, that's why I came there," he said, trying to get her to believe him.

"That's why you came? You came to me, to us, because you felt guilty?" she asked.

"No, I wanted to be with you, comfort you, support you, and, when I got there, I realised how stupid I'd been, realised how much I'd let you all down," he replied.

"But you carried on as if it hadn't happened, you didn't bat an eyelid, you were just normal," she replied.

"I wanted to forget it ever happened. I wanted to get her out of my head, and just lose that feeling and be with you. I only want you," Connor said.

Becks' expression twisted into a blend of fury, with frustration, revulsion, and loathing etched on her features.

"And what did you say to her when you were having sex with her? Were you saying how much you wanted her?" Becks asked.

"NO! We didn't even talk, there were no words between us, it was just physical, stupid, animal behaviour," he proclaimed.

"Animal? She really did get to you, didn't she? She lit a fire in you that I've never been able to do?" Becks responded.

"No matter what I say, you won't believe me. So, I know I just have to prove it to you, and I'll wait, I'll do whatever it takes," Connor replied.

"Do you blame me for not believing you? You've broken my heart, our trust, our marriage, and I have to live with this now, forever. This is now my life because of you," she cried.

"Becks, please," he pleaded, as he walked towards her.

"I can't keep doing this. Just, do me a favour, and don't come in here every night, not for now, please," Becks asked.

"OK, I'll go. Please, know how much I love you," he replied lovingly, in desperation.

"If you loved me, you wouldn't have even looked at her," she said, with such disappointment in her voice. He turned around, walked out into the hallway, and closed the bedroom door. Once more, he found himself engulfed in a night of disappointment, regret, and guilt, unable to envision any possible solution.

The following morning, Becks bounced back, brushed herself off, and headed to school with determination and strength. By 9:30 am she got a call. It was great news, the potential tenants adored the house and were eager to sign a twelve-month lease. This brought a mix of joy and relief to Becks.

Connor's phone rang at 11:32 am. It was the clinic delivering more positive news. His tests came back clear, and since he didn't exhibit any other symptoms, they discharged him.

Later that evening, Connor entered the house with a beaming smile and a bouquet for Becks, and shared the good news from his day.

"Hi, so, today was a good day. These are for you my love," he said to Becks, as he handed her the bunch of roses.

"Thank you, they're beautiful. Yes, a good day. I'm relieved the house is being rented, it's a huge weight from my mind, at least we can get some rent in," Becks replied.

"Yes, me too, and guess what? I didn't want to tell you over the phone. My test results came back clear, too. That's also good news. A great day all around," he said, as he attempted to feel some warmth from Becks.

With a shocked and almost disappointed look on her face, she responded with a strained smile, "Yes, yes of course it is, I'm pleased for you." Yet inside, she was filled with disappointment and confusion. Did she wish for her husband to have a sexually transmitted infection? Absolutely not, however, she couldn't shake the feeling that he was getting off too lightly with everything that had happened.

As the night fell, Becks lay in bed, completely absorbed in her laptop. Suddenly, Connor entered the room, headed to the bathroom to change into his pyjamas, then made his way to the bed and climbed in on his side, exuding the excitement of a playful schoolboy.

"What are you doing?" Becks asked.

"I'm coming to bed," he replied.

"You're not sleeping in here," she replied forcefully.

"Why? You said you couldn't be with me until I got the all clear, and I'm clear," he said, confused and disgruntled.

"You just don't understand, do you? Do you think it's that easy? Just because you're not strutting around with the latest STI, doesn't mean I can just forgive you and we can move on from this," she said sternly.

"Oh, I'm sorry. I just thought—" he said.

But Becks interrupted him, "Well, you thought wrong. I'm sorry, I'm not ready yet. I need time, and you need to be patient," she exclaimed.

"Yes, I'm sorry, I didn't think," he replied, as he pulled the covers off himself and got out of bed.

He walked towards the door and turned back around. "I thought you would be happy," he said, as he looked lovingly at her.

"How can I be happy? My husband, the father of my children, has been to the clap clinic to get tested for an STI, because he shagged what we now know to be the local bike, who also turned out to be a psychopath. Oh, and not forgetting that you've also killed this woman, and I've helped bury her body under the patio of our old house! Please, tell me where I'm going wrong?" she proclaimed sarcastically.

"How are we ever going to move on if you're like this?" he asked.

"So now this is my fault for taking too long to forgive you? Am I understanding your question right?" she asked back.

"No, I didn't mean it like that. I just want us to go back to the way it was. I miss you, you're my wife," he replied.

"Yes. I'm your wife, but where was that sentiment when you were with her? Where is my respect?" she asked, sitting herself upright in bed.

"I do respect you; you're the most wonderful woman I've ever known. You're amazing," he replied, walking towards her.

"You fucked all the respect you had for me when you fucked her!" she said with resentment.

She couldn't help but feel angry at herself every time she cursed, but her feelings were overpowering.

"Becks, please, I was weak, OK. I was a weak, weak man. It doesn't mean I don't love you. It doesn't mean I don't respect you or want you. I stupidly got my head turned and I regret it, I regret it so much," he replied, with such sincerity in his voice.

"I know, but that doesn't help me. Those images of you in that hotel bed, seeing you naked, lying there, knowing that you had just had sex with another woman, my imagination is running away with me, envisioning you and her together. It makes me sick! And you, you risked everything, our entire life together, and you didn't care. Do you have any idea how that feels? I know, it's boring. Do you think I enjoy getting up at 6 am every morning, sorting the boys, putting my happy face on, going to work and acting like everything's OK? I also have a stressful job,

I'm also the boss, but nothing ever happens to the boss. We're strong and fearless, and I have to get on with it. Day in and day out I put on a smile and I perform. I perform my duties as a mother, as a wife, and as a head teacher. I do the lot. And yes, it's boring, it's routine, but it's a life. It was our life, the life we chose together. Everything since university, everything that we ever dreamed of, has come true, and you go and ruin it all for a fumble!" she continued emotionally. As she began to cry, her voice broke under the strain. Recognising the need for her to release her frustration, Connor wisely refrained from interrupting and remained silent. Becks paused for a minute.

"What do you want me to do? Tell me what can I do?" he begged.

"I don't know. I wish I knew. You've made me say things this week I've never said. I've cursed and used words I never use because I hate that common behaviour, and you've belittled me into this way of thinking!" she exclaimed.

"Shall we go and see a therapist?" he suggested.

"No! I don't need to pay a stranger to listen to me and then tell me I'm angry at you. I know how I feel about you. If it wasn't for those beautiful, innocent boys in there, I would leave you, I would be out of that door. I don't need you to live my life, I'm more than capable of supporting myself. I'm with you because I want to be with you. Well, I wanted to," she said, as her emotions exploded.

Rivulets of tears streamed down her cheeks, prompting her to shield her face with her hands while she dabbed at the tears and let out a heavy gulp.

"I'll do anything and I promise, I'll make this up to you. I'll work every day of my life to make up for what I've done. I love you, I love our boys, I love our little family and I never want to lose you," Connor said, as he approached her and perched on the side of the bed.

Clueless and torn, he grappled with uncertainty, yearning to embrace her, yet fearing the repercussions. Every move he made seemed to irk her, intensifying his dilemma.

"You could have got her pregnant, did you ever think of that? If all this hadn't happened, you could have got her pregnant, did that even cross your mind?" she asked him.

"She was on birth control," he said quickly and quietly.

Becks smirked, "Wow. I thought there were no words between you?" she asked harshly.

"No, there wasn't. I asked her and that's what she said," he replied.

"Right, so before you went in, you asked that question? God, you're a fucking pig! I hate you. I can't stand to look at you! I just don't understand, you're such a snob, usually. You look down on women who flaunt their bodies and flirt to get attention. You hate those fake-looking women, so what was it about her? What made her so irresistible to you?" she replied with utter hatred in her voice.

He nodded his head, "You're right, I would never entertain a woman like that. I just don't know. Perhaps her forward nature, I have no explanation," he replied.

"And did you not think that the random woman who walks into the men's changing room and into a shower block where a man is showering, she's what, a saint? How did you know she was telling you the truth? You're so stupid. Do you think that highly of yourself? Did you honestly think you were her first? You didn't know this woman and yet you had sex with her, without protecting yourself, protecting me. You jeopardised everything we've worked for, for a few minutes of pleasure." Becks paused.

"Becks, I—"

"Wait, was that the night that you pulled my hair out?" she asked, interrupting him.

"No. It was the night that you got upset with me because I said no to you," he responded.

"Right, when I was in the shower. So, you'd had your fun in the gym shower with her, and then came home to boring old me, because, let's face it, I'm not 'shagging in the shower' material, am I?" she said sarcastically.

"I felt guilty. I felt terrible for what I'd done and I just couldn't then be with you, it didn't seem fair," he answered.

"Fair! None of this is fair, not one element of this is fair. So, what was the hair-pulling all about, had you slept with her then?" she asked.

"No, that was the night I met her, briefly. She came over, flirted and then sent me some naked pictures of herself and, I'm not going to lie, it turned me on, and I took that out on you," he said, ashamed of his behaviour.

"And you then go and act like a fifteen-year-old boy and use her pictures to masturbate to, am I getting this right?" she asked.

"Yes! Like a stupid, horny idiot, yes, I did that, and I'm disgusted with myself for being so bloody pathetic. I don't know how many more times I can say sorry. I promise, you know everything, I'm trying to be transparent. I fucked up. I've royally fucked this up, but I don't want this to end. I love you, I want you," he replied, as he got down on his knees.

"I just don't know how to overcome what's happened in the last five days. I was happy, I was content and I thought you were, too. I thought we were on the same page, we never argued. We've never gone head-to-head like this in all the years we've been together. Then, this one woman walks into our lives and, bang, it's all gone. I never believed we were that weak. I can't begin to tell you how disappointed I am. I feel like I don't know you anymore," she said, with sadness etched on her face.

"Let me try. Please, let me try and make this up to you. Somehow, I will," he begged. She nodded her head, and he walked on his knees towards her.

"Can I sleep here, please?" he asked desperately.

"Yes, whatever, but nothing will happen. I'm not ready, so don't push me!" she replied hesitantly.

As the sun rose, Becks awoke with a heavy sense of fatigue. Throughout the night, she deliberately faced away from Connor, lying on her left side to ensure there was no hint of warmth or affection between them. She felt drained and unsure of how to regain her energy. With only a few friends, none of whom she felt comfortable confiding in, she experienced a deep sense of loneliness and desperation. All she longed for was a glimmer of hope to bring back a sense of happiness to her life. She went downstairs to find Connor feeding the boys.

"Good morning, Mummy," Connor said. Becks smiled and ran her fingers through Logan's hair, smiling at them.

"Right, let's get to school. Go up and brush your teeth," she said, as she forced a smile from her mouth. The boys ran upstairs.

"I'm going to take the boys to my parent's house this weekend, you can stay here," Becks said to Connor.

"Can I come too, please? Let's make a weekend out of it" he asked.

"Fine, just pay attention to the environment, and please, don't push me," she said.

"I promise, I just want to be with you all," he said.

Friday evening marked the beginning of their journey as they embarked on a lengthy drive, making a pit stop at the motorway services to eat dinner. The boys gleefully played arcade games while the car recharged, filling the air with laughter and joy. Becks yearned for the return of that sense of security she once knew. As they reached the farm, a heartfelt reception awaited them. Bob's recovery was progressing, but he still had a long way to go before resuming full responsibility for the farm. Later that evening, they gathered around the familiar dining table with Becks' siblings, parents, and Julie, reminiscing about their childhood experiences on the farm. However, Becks seemed distant, lost in her thoughts.

The conversations continued in the background, but all she could perceive was a blur of indistinct sounds.

"What do you think, Becks?" Jason asked.

"What? Sorry, I was miles away. What did you say?" Becks asked.

"Julie wants a horse-drawn carriage to get to the church," Jason said.

"Yes, that sounds beautiful. Will you use one of your own horses?" Becks asked, in an attempt to reconnect herself back to the conversation.

"Yes, she has someone who'll drive the carriage for her," Jason added.

"That sounds lovely. Have you set a date?" Becks asked.

"Yeah, did you not hear? Set for 19 June, next year," Jason replied.

"Sorry, I think I'm just tired, it's been a hectic week. I think I might go to bed, guys," Becks said.

"Yes, you go up love, you look tired," Joan replied, with a concerned look. Becks smiled warmly at her mother

"Goodnight, everyone," Becks said, as she stood up and hugged her mum.

"I'll come with you," Connor said, as he started to stand up.

"No! You stay for a while, I'm fine," Becks replied rapidly, as everyone looked at her and wondered what was wrong.

"I'm tired, too. I think a good rest will do us all good," Connor replied. Together, they walked upstairs and entered Becks' former room where the boys were already fast asleep on their mattresses.

After changing into her pyjamas she lay in bed, gazing up at the ceiling.

"That was nice," Connor said.

"Yes, it was. Dad seemed happy and so did Mum. I'm pleased," Becks replied.

"Becks, you're so far away, what can I do to make this better? What if we moved? What if we came over this way, started again, a fresh start?" he asked.

"As lovely as that sounds, our entire lives are in Milton, your firm, my job, the kids' school, our house that was meant to be our fresh start. All we would be doing is moving out of Milton and bringing our problems with us," she replied.

"But the boys love it here, we could get some land. It would be nice to be free," he said positively.

"Why? Are you not free, now? What's holding you?" she asked.

"I didn't mean it like that. I just meant a change, the outdoors, the countryside, maybe it would be a positive change," he continued to suggest.

"I was happy. I have a job I love, well, used to love. Everything that's wrong is because of your actions because of what you did. Moving away from our home is not the answer. And remember, we can never sell that other house, not in our lifetime. That's a noose around our necks for the rest of our lives," she said quietly.

"It was just an idea," he replied sheepishly.

"And what are you going to do with land? You hate this part of my family; you hate their simplicity. What, do you think moving to the country side will, what, make you less stuck up? It's a bad idea. Goodnight, I need to sleep," she said, turning her back. As he sat up, a wave of confusion and annoyance washed over him. Each word he uttered seemed to grate on her nerves.

A whole four weeks had gone by in the blink of an eye. Signs of summer were everywhere, with bursts of colour, and the sun shining bright. The new tenants had settled in and they had finally received a rent payment. Becks was beginning to feel a bit more upbeat. Connor stepped up as the perfect husband. He was attentive, assisting with the boys, and spending quality time with them outside of work hours.

Becks continued to keep her distance physically from him, however she focused on moving forward with a positive attitude. Despite her efforts, she couldn't shake off the betrayal and deceit that lingered in her mind, making it difficult for her to see him as her husband. Yet, she could sense an emotional bond forming slowly once more, as long as she persisted in maintaining a positive mindset. Connor displayed remarkable patience throughout the process which helped Becks to heal. The gym was a distant memory for Connor. Determined to give his family the best, he invested all his energy into them, never missing a chance to be home on time every evening, cherishing every moment they spent together.

As the sun continued to beam down on a warm Tuesday evening in early July, the clock struck 6 pm and the doorbell echoed through the house. Connor, leaving the delicious aroma of Becks' cooking in the kitchen, made his way to the door. To his surprise, two unfamiliar men dressed in sharp suits stood before him, their purpose unknown.

"Good evening, Mr Jones?" the man asked.

"Yes. How can I help?" Connor asked.

"I'm Detective Sergeant John McCabe and this is Police Constable Alex King, may we come inside for a minute?" the detective asked, as they flashed their badges.

"Yes, of course, please come in," Connor answered, leading them to living room.

"Please, have a seat. Is it just me, or do you need to see my wife also? Connor asked.

"Yes, if she's available, that would help," the detective replied. The officers sat down and gazed around Connor and Becks' idyllic home, while Connor went to Becks in the kitchen.

"The police are here," Connor whispered, as he grabbed Becks' hands.

"No, no, please, no," Becks whispered in a panic.

"Be calm, stick to the story," Connor whispered back, as he stared into her eyes and nodded his head. Becks nodded back and inhaled deeply.

Detective McCabe, standing at around five-feet eleven inches tall, had a noticeable round belly that made him seem even taller. With a moustache and jet-black hair, his appearance was distinct. His deep, brown eyes bore into those he spoke to, as if peering deep into their soul. When he spoke, his clear voice commanded the attention of the room, giving off an aura that made it feel like everyone was presumed guilty until proven innocent. Whereas PC King, a slight, slender figure, clearly inexperienced in his position, had acne marks on his face which made his visual appearance all the more naive. He sported a classic, short haircut that was gelled intently. He seemed out of place in his suit, almost like a child playing dress up.

Connor and Becks made their way back into the living room.

"This is my wife, Rebecca. Can we get you some tea, officers?" Connor asked.

"No, thank you. We just have a few questions, if you don't mind?" Detective McCabe asked.

"Yes, of course," Connor replied.

"We're investigating the disappearance of Kerry Reed. We believe she was a tenant of yours from January to May of this year, is that correct?" the detective asked.

"Yes, that's correct, she moved out around late May. We had a little trouble with her as she'd stopped paying the rent. We unfortunately had to take legal action, but then, out of the blue, she messaged my wife and said that she was sorry for not paying and she was leaving. We both went to the property, and she gave us the keys back and left. We haven't seen or heard from her since," Connor said, as Becks nodded in agreement.

"OK. We have statements from her friends saying that they're worried about her and it's not like her to just disappear. We've also spoken to her husband, who has advised us that this is not the first time she's gone 'off the radar', shall we say, but not for this long, according to a friend of hers," the detective continued.

"I'm sorry, we don't know any more. She didn't leave a forwarding address with us, and, if I'm honest, we're just grateful to have the house back. It was a stressful time for us," Connor replied.

"Of course, So, just to confirm, you were both there at the house when she left?" the officer asked.

"Yes, it was a Saturday night, I can't remember the date, but yes, both my wife and I were there. We thought it best that we go together and, like I said, we've not heard anything since," Connor repeated, as Becks smiled and nodded again.

"OK, thank you. Well, if anything else comes to mind, or you remember anything else, please do get in touch. Here's my card," Detective McCabe said, as he stood up and buttoned his suit jacket.

"Yes, of course, I hope she turns up safe," Connor said.

"Yes, so do we. Thanks again for your time," the detective said, walking out of the door. Connor closed the door behind them.

"Oh my God!" Becks said in a panic.

"Be quiet, just calm down. Listen, you heard him, she does this all the time, you need to relax," Connor replied quietly, in an attempt to reassure his wife.

Once the officers had driven off, Becks served dinner, but she had no appetite. Her mind was racing, filled with worry. After putting the boys to bed, she sat staring into space. She felt scared. Just when she thought she was making progress, she had to confront the past all over again, feeling like she was back at square one. That night, as they lay in bed, Becks found herself staring up at the ceiling.

"Are you OK?" Connor asked.

"No! I can't go over all of this again, I just can't. What if they know something?" Becks said.

"We know where she is. If something had happened at the house, people are living there now, we would be the first to know," Connor stated rationally.

"But what if they know it wasn't her dropping off the car, I'm scared. I'm so scared," Becks repeated in a high-pitched voice.

"Come here, everything will be fine. The chances are they'll come back and question me again. I'm sure my relationship with her will come up and I'm ready for that, but you shouldn't have to answer anything else and, if you do, she texted you, we went, she left, end of story," Connor replied logically. Becks gave a nod of agreement and embraced him tightly, seeking solace in his presence as the pain overwhelmed her. The anguish was crippling.

As the weekend came to a close, Connor and Becks carried on with their usual routine, unaware that the police had yet to reach out to them again. Little did they suspect that behind closed doors, a thorough investigation was underway. Unbeknownst to them, Connor's photograph had made its way onto the police investigation board, alongside Alan, Geoff, and several other individuals connected to Kerry.

"Good morning team. We have a potential missing person, a Kerry Reed, age thirty-seven. Her husband, Michael Reed, age forty-one and daughter Darcy, age twelve, two of her friends, John Walker, age thirty-nine, known to us for drug possession, and Sophie Meaden age thirty-seven, also known to the police for drug possession, have reported Kerry Reed missing, stating that they haven't heard from her in over four weeks, which is not like her, apparently. Mrs Reed is going through a divorce, which has been slow, for almost three years. They have been back and forth through the courts, and they are still to conclude legally. Mrs Reed is still legally married to Michael Reed and it certainly appears there's no love lost there. Mr Reed seems to have washed his hands of her for being so unreliable and, as he called it, abandoning their daughter several times. There also appears to be a pattern of blackmail going on. Mrs Reed's laptop was at Miss Meaden's apartment, and we've uncovered that she was blackmailing several men, specifically targeting married men, age range, late thirties to late fifties. All of these men have one thing in common, money and a second home. Mrs Reed seems to take tenancy at their rental property, form a relationship with the husband and then blackmail them into paying their own rent. You can see several faces up here, she had indecent images of them which I'm guessing was used as evidence to get them to pay up. Mrs Reed was obviously not liked by these men and was last seen on Saturday, 25 May, where she apparently left her latest rental home in Tree Hill, this home belonging to Connor and Rebecca Jones. She had images of Mr Jones, these were found on her computer, which were taken a few weeks prior to her disappearance. She was seen driving away from the rental property at around 5:30 pm on that Saturday evening. Is there any more information gained on that?" Detective McCabe asked.

"Yes, sir. The last three people to see her were, Andrew Smith and Wayne Bolton, the two men who took her car at The Cash Car Mobile Site on Gillford Trading Estate on Saturday 25 May. She sold her Mercedes and then took a taxi back towards the rental house estate," Officer King stated.

"What did these two men have to say? Any CCTV?" McCabe asked.

"They both said it was a very quick exchange, she accepted the offer that they gave. She had her driving licence, a bank statement, a copy of her husband's passport and, apparently, he'd sent an email permitting her to sell the car, as it was in his name. I've questioned Mr Reed on this and he denies sending that email so it appears that Mrs Reed has created a faux email address and fraudulently given permission. They showed me all the documents, and her signature on the iPad matched her signature on her passport. Mr Smith and Mr Bolton both said she was fine, chatty even. Unfortunately, they erased all CCTV – it's routinely done every four weeks – so we have no visual, but they did confirm that there was nothing suspicious," Officer King concluded.

"It doesn't make any sense; we're missing something. Perhaps one of the other men got hold of her, have we checked alibis for all the other gentlemen?" McCabe asked.

"Yes, sir, two were out of the country and all the others have solid alibis," Officer King replied.

Detective McCabe was baffled by the events leading up to her disappearance.

"The last person to see her was Tamur Khan, age forty-three, the taxi driver who drove her back towards Tree Hill on that same Saturday evening. He collected her at 6:30 pm, he told us that she asked to be dropped off on the side of the road, paid cash and walked down the hill back towards the housing estate. He did not drop her at a house. We have no CCTV in that area and no doorbell camera footage either, she just disappears. If you look here, you can see the taxi drive into the estate at 6:44 pm, we lose eyes on the taxi and Mrs Reed, and then he drives back out onto the main road at 6:46 pm. Since then, we've had no sightings of her, and no further movement on bank accounts where the £18,500 for the Mercedes was paid into. She did, however, book a one way flight to Majorca for Sunday morning. This was booked on Friday at 7:37 pm via her phone using her credit card, but she never got on that flight and seems to have just disappeared into thin air. We've been house-to-house on the estate to see if she had any friends, but she wasn't known to anyone by name. The only witness we have is Nigel Collins, who lives opposite the house that she was renting. He confirmed he saw her drive off wearing a black baseball cap and sunglasses on Saturday 25 May at around 5:30 pm. He also confirmed that both Mr and Mrs Jones were at the property when Mrs Reed drove off," Officer King said.

"OK, why did she go back that way, did she go back to the house? Where are her belongings? Let's bring Mr Jones in for questioning. Let's see what he says about this affair and go from there. She has not just vanished! Let's also get Mr Khan back in, since he was the last one to visually see her, and there's no proof that she got out of the taxi. Did he have any further pick-ups after he claimed to drop her off? We need to take a look inside his cab and his house," Detective McCabe said.

"Do you think that he didn't drop her where he said he did?" Officer King asked.

"It's a possibility; did you ask what he did after he made the drop?" McCabe asked.

"No, but I can ring the taxi firm and confirm his movements after this job," Officer King suggested.

"OK, great work. Let's get this info and get them in for questioning," Detective McCabe ordered.

An hour later Officer King knocked on McCabe's office door.

"Sir, we have some developments. So, according to the taxi firm, Tamur Khan clocked off at 6.48 pm and, from the GPS, returned straight home. He apparently lives alone, in a small bedsit. He's married, but his wife and children live in Pakistan. He didn't log back on until the following morning at 10:30 am," Officer King stated.

"OK, why did he clock off so quickly, was he due to finish?" Detective McCabe asked.

"They're self-employed with this firm sir, so it means they can clock on and off as they wish, there's no finish time for their shift," Officer King stated.

"OK, get him in. I want his car and his house searched, look for anything that may belong to Kerry Reed, get on it now. I'll go to the Jones's again and get Connor Jones in for questioning," Detective McCabe ordered once again.

At 5:30 pm on Saturday, the doorbell suddenly chimed, interrupting Becks' cooking session. Startled, she glanced over at Connor with wide eyes. A mix of panic and curiosity filled the room.

"It's OK," he whispered. He opened the door to Detective McCabe and another officer that he didn't recognise.

"Good evening, Detective," Connor said.

"Mr Jones, we were wondering if you could join us at the station? We have a few questions for you," Detective McCabe requested.

"Yes, of course, am I under arrest?" Connor asked.

"No, Mr Jones, we just have a few more questions for you," the detective answered. With his coat in hand, Connor made his way towards Becks, who wore a look of pure terror on her face. He leaned in and placed a soft kiss on her cheek,

"Don't worry, I won't be long," he whispered.

As Connor hopped into the police car, they drove to the nearby police station. Upon arrival, he was guided through the back entrance and led to an interview room, where the recording began. After the customary introductions for the tape, McCabe began his interrogation.

"Mr Jones, can you explain the nature of your relationship with Mrs Reed? We have reason to believe that you were romantically involved, could you kindly tell us about this," Detective McCabe asked.

"It wasn't a romantic relationship, it wasn't a relationship, it was sex. I, we, slept together a few times but that was it, nothing romantically linked," Connor explained calmly.

"So, a sexual encounter is not a romantic encounter in your opinion Mr Jones?" the detective asked.

"It wasn't an affair, I didn't love her, I didn't date her. It was sex and only a couple of times, each time unplanned, and there were no organised meetings," Connor replied.

"Can you give us details of how you met Mrs Reed, and how and where these encounters took place?" McCabe asked, trying his best to sniff out a rat.

"Yes, and, for the tape, my wife knows about this. It was a mistake and it shouldn't have happened. I first met Kerry at the gym, several months back in January. I didn't know that she was the tenant in our rental property, my wife handled all of that. She introduced herself to me as Suzy, not Kerry. After seeing her there, she started flirting with me, and then somehow got my name and messaged me on social media. I'll admit, I was intrigued, I'm not going to lie, she's pretty attractive, and sexy, and I was flattered. A few days later she came onto me at the gym and I didn't resist. That was the first time and I felt guilty about it. My wife is a very good lady and I've never done anything like this before," he explained.

"OK, so when did you find out that she was your tenant?" the detective asked.

"She stopped paying rent in March. Becks, my wife, was beside herself with worry. This Kerry, or Suzy, whatever her name is, had given Becks a sob story just before Christmas. She'd told Becks that her husband was abusive and that she was desperate to get away from him and she needed to get out of the house. The estate agent messed up with the paper work and, long story short, Becks ended up giving her the keys out of the goodness of her heart. She paid the deposit and a month's rent upfront. Becks thought she was OK, she appeared very together, wealthy, she was always well-groomed and well-dressed, and Becks thought she was good for the payments. Plus, she used her daughter as a pawn; Becks, she's a teacher, she would help anyone in need. Kerry then paid, I think, maybe two more payments, and then just stopped responding to Becks. Becks contacted the estate agent and they then realised that they had forgotten to do the checks, but by that time it was too late. We then had to take her to court to evict her. During this time Suzy and I had met a couple more times, it was never planned, I don't even have the woman's phone number," Connor continued. Without pausing for a breath, he effortlessly spun a tangled web of lies from his lips.

Detective McCabe was visibly stunned, nearly at a loss for words, as Connor kept rambling on, his expression reflecting his surprise at the sheer volume of information being divulged.

"So, you were sleeping with this woman but yet you didn't have her phone number?" the detective asked.

"I wasn't sleeping with her. The first time, she came into the shower when I was in there at the gym, and she pounced on me. I'm not proud, but I'm a bloke. If any woman does that, you know, it's hard to say no. I got carried away and I can't explain why, I mean, you've seen pictures, you know, she is good-looking," he said, blushing slightly.

"Yes, we've seen pictures, Mr Jones," McCabe said.

"The second time, I'm guessing you'll be able to see from her social media messages, she lured me to the Empress Hotel in town. You'll also see that I messaged her asking her to stop and to leave me alone. I love my wife and my boys, and I just wanted her to stop, so I went there and, again, it's like she had me under a spell. We had sex in the hotel room and I fell asleep. When I woke up, she was gone," Connor said innocently.

He made a concerted effort to portray himself as the victim as he continued his web of lies.

"That same day my father-in-law had a heart attack, so I left to go and be with my wife. They live north of here and it's a couple of hour's drive away. I deleted everything to do with that social media account and haven't been back on since. I came home after a few days away; we stayed at my in-laws. It was half term, so Becks and the boys stayed at her parents' house and I came back alone, it was midweek, I think. When I arrived home, unbeknown to me, Suzy had been watching me. She knew where I lived, which I had never told her by the way, and I still to this day don't know how she knew. She knocked on the door and barged into my house. I told her to leave, I begged her, but she came on to me again and I caved. I had no strength to say no to her and I hate myself for it," he continued. In a masterful display of manipulation, he adeptly orchestrated a narrative where he played the role of the victim, all the while harbouring a profound awareness of his guilt.

McCabe's face displayed a perplexed expression. He couldn't shake off the unsettling feeling that something was amiss.

"So, you had sex with her in your house, Mr Jones?" McCabe asked.

"Yes, but she left straight after. There was no talking, no conversation, it was just physical those three times, nothing else," he confirmed.

"And then you found out at court that she was your tenant?" the detective asked.

"Yes, the court date was, I'm sorry the dates are muddled in my head, I think a couple of weeks or so later. I hadn't heard from her or seen her since the time she came to the house. She walked into the courtroom and smirked at me. I panicked, I couldn't believe it, I was confused, it couldn't have been a coincidence," Connor innocently said.

"You must have been angry, Mr Jones?" McCabe asked, as he squinted his eyes at Connor.

"I was surprised. I wasn't angry, just confused, so, after court, I went over to the rental house and I confronted her. It was then that she asked me for money. She blackmailed me, saying that she would tell Becks, and showed me a picture of me sleeping at the hotel on her phone. What choice did I have? So, I went and got her the money, and I gave it to her on the same day, that Monday, I can get you the dates. She said she would pay the money to Becks as rent, but she didn't," Connor explained. Although he typically shied away from lengthy oratory, he found himself compelled to talk to avoid questions. He believed if he continued speaking he could outsmart the detectives. So much so, that he even surprised himself with the eloquence of the untruths that he was articulating.

"Did it not get heated when she didn't pay you the rent, Mr Jones?" McCabe asked.

"No, it didn't. I mean, how stupid is this system? So, I'm an honest man, right? I work an honest job, I've gone to college, worked hard to achieve. I want a better retirement, so I invest in property, then someone comes along and decides they aren't going to pay the rent, so I'm screwed. I then have to wait two months for them not to pay me my money, then I can go to court, but I have to wait another six to eight weeks for the court date. If it goes in my favour, they have another month to vacate my property. That's six months with no rent, and they get away with this. If I went now to a shop and stole a loaf of bread worth, what, £1.80, you would throw the book at me, but people like this, who know the system, play the system and rip off decent hard-working people, it's wrong!" he passionately exclaimed, as he pointed his finger down on the desk.

It was evident to McCabe that Connor was becoming increasingly agitated. He eagerly awaited the opportunity for Connor to slip up and disclose information by constantly goading him.

"You seem annoyed, Mr Jones?" the detective asked.

"I'm not annoyed; I'm disappointed with the system. Anyway, I'm going off track. So, by Friday she'd not paid the money to Becks. The judge at court said that she had to pay by Friday or the eviction notice would go live, so I went back to the house on the Friday after work. I sat and had a heart-to-heart with her, the first time we had spoken properly. I begged her to leave and forget what had happened. I told her to keep the money, but please, just go, and she agreed. She said something about going away, a fresh start, she said she was tired of it all, whatever that meant. She sent a message to Becks asking her to meet her on Saturday, and she apologised and told us that she was moving out. I thanked her, nothing else physical happened, I swear. So, that night, I sat Becks down and told her the truth, I owned up to my mistake. She was mad at me, but she wanted this house business sorting. So, on Saturday Becks and I went over together. It was awkward, we didn't speak about what had gone on. Kerry, or Suzy, apologised to Becks and she got in her car and drove off. My old neighbour, Nigel, saw her drive away on Saturday, and that's the last we saw of her. Becks and I then cleaned the house over the weekend, and I had to grovel. I've not heard from her since," Connor said, as he took a deep breath.

McCabe found himself puzzled once more, questioning why someone would confess to an affair when there was a chance the other person might walk away.

"OK. Mr Jones, that was a very detailed account, thank you. Your neighbour, Nigel, has confirmed that he saw Mrs Reed drive away and that you and Mrs Jones were at the house when she did so. What I can't understand is if Mrs Reed was leaving, why didn't she just give you the keys? And why then tell your wife about the affair?" McCabe asked.

"I was protecting myself. I knew that this woman was volatile. If I'd asked for the keys on Friday, she might have got annoyed. I had just managed to get through to her, appeal to her better nature, shall we say. She could have set me up, lured me in again. How did I know that she wasn't getting Becks there on the Saturday to tell her? It could have been a trap. So, I did the hardest thing and I owned up. I respect my wife and I wanted it to come from me. Besides, as you asked, if she was leaving, she could have just given me the keys, but she asked to see Becks and I didn't trust her. I didn't want to aggravate the situation any more than it already was," Connor replied rationally.

"Fair point, Mr Jones. Was there any threatening behaviour? Any arguments between you and Mrs Reed, Mr Jones?" McCabe inquired.

"No, it was very amicable. I'm not an aggressive person; I try to live my life calmly and avoid drama. I know now that she hunted me, she knew who I was. I believe she knew exactly what she was doing and she knew how to blackmail me. I told her that I'd told Becks when we arrived at the house on Saturday, and I guess she had no place to stand; she couldn't blackmail me anymore," Connor concluded.

The logic behind Connor's account was undeniable, indicating that he'd mentally rehearsed this particular moment numerous times.

"Yes, it appears you were not the only one she was doing this to, Mr Jones. We've located her computer which was at a friend's house. It had several pictures of different men, including you, Mr Jones, which could be used as a potential motive to harm Mrs Reed. We're looking into each case individually. It just so happens that you were the last, gentleman friend, shall we say, to see her," the detective said.

"I wasn't the only one? What was she doing, sleeping with other men and then blackmailing them too?" he asked. The way he spoke made him seem as if he'd been violated.

"It appears so, Mr Jones. She also sold her car and booked a flight, however, she never got on the plane, hence why we're investigating," the detective said.

"What was her name to all these other men? She told me her name was Suzy and her social media profile was Suzy T, but she told my wife her name was Kerry. The photocopy of her passport said Kerry Reed, but perhaps she left using another name?" Connor confidently insinuated.

"So, you saw her passport, Mr Jones?" the detective asked.

"Yes, after the court date. My wife had initially taken a copy of her passport, but I hadn't checked it prior, I didn't see the need.

I only checked after the court day. I went to our office at home and saw for myself that her name wasn't Suzy, or was it?" Connor answered, smirking.

With no way forward, McCabe had to swallow his pride and acknowledge that he'd reached a dead end.

"Thank you, Mr Jones, for clarifying and for giving us a very detailed encounter. So, the house she was living in, has it been rented out again, Mr Jones?" the detective asked.

"Yes. We got in as quick as we could, cleaned up, freshened the paint and rented it back out," Connor replied.

"And was there anything left behind? Anything that might help, documents, etc.?" the detective asked.

"No. A couple of items of clothing, some food left in the cupboards, but nothing with any details on. I'm sorry I can't help any more. I hope you find her but, I won't lie, I'll be glad if I never see her again. If she ever does get in touch, I'll be sure to let you know," Connor said convincingly.

"OK, Mr Jones, thank you for your time. I'm hoping we won't need to bother you again," Detective McCabe said, as he stood up and held out his hand.

Standing tall and composed, Connor neatly tucked in his polo shirt and adjusted his glasses, exuding a nerdy image. He greeted the officer with a firm handshake, and confidently made his way out.

"What do you think, boss?" Officer King asked.

"He's been caught with his trousers down. It's clear he's not very competent, just spewing out words without any thought. I've never seen anyone talk so much during an interview before," Detective McCabe answered, looking down at the file with his right hand in his pocket.

"Right, let's get talking to this taxi driver," Detective McCabe said.

"Yes, boss, the officers are at his house now. They'll search the premises and his car," Officer King stated.

"Great, can we also run a data check on any Susie T, Suzy T, Susan T and Sue T, that left the country on that Sunday. Let's see if anything crops up," the detective asked.

"That could be a lot of data, sir," Officer King replied.

"Yes, as much as I don't like to admit it, Jones had a point. She was possibly using a fake name, different ID, it's worth a look," McCabe replied.

Connor walked out of the police station and called Becks.

"Can you pick me up?" he asked.

"Yes, have they let you go? I've been going out of my mind," Becks asked.

"Of course they have. I'll start walking towards the precinct, everything is fine, relax," Connor said reassuringly. Within ten minutes, Becks had arrived with the boys in the car. Connor got into the passenger seat,

"What did they say?" Becks asked.

"We'll talk at home," Connor replied.

The boys were completely absorbed in their iPads sitting in the back seats. The drive back home was filled with silence, and Becks began to feel a sense of unease creeping in. Finally, they arrived and parked the car on the driveway.

"Get the boys settled and come back down," Connor said. Becks took the boys upstairs.

"How about we just have PJ's tonight? We'll give you a really good scrub tomorrow," Becks said, embracing her sons lovingly. With excited agreement from both boys, it wasn't long until they were asleep in their beds.

Becks made her way downstairs and found Connor in the kitchen, clenching a bottle of beer.

"We need to talk about this," Becks said. He took her by the hand and walked her outside to the garden.

"Where's your phone?" he asked.

"Upstairs," she replied.

"OK, come outside," Connor said. They walked briskly to the top corner of the garden,

"I don't know if I'm paranoid, but I don't want us to talk about anything inside. I'm sure it's nothing, but we need to be extra careful," Connor said cautiously.

"Do you think they've bugged the house?" Panic was evident on Becks' face as she anxiously inquired.

"No, I'm sure they haven't, but just in case. They let me go and there's no follow-up. Nigel has confirmed that we were both at the house when she drove off, but you need to stick to this story if they ask you, OK? I think they're going to look into the taxi driver that picked you up. They know she came back towards the house," Connor continued.

"I left a hair bobble in the taxi – it was Kerry's – I wanted to leave some evidence of hers that showed she'd been in the car. Did I do right?" Becks asked.

"Are you kidding? That's genius! Hopefully, they'll find it, and that puts us in the clear. God, you're amazing," he expressed with gratitude.

He proceeded to disclose to her the precise details of his conversation with the police, ensuring that Becks was fully informed about his confession regarding the affair.

"From this point on, we don't speak about this again. We have to put this to bed, move forward," Connor said.

"I thought that was it. I thought it was all over, I was petrified. I can't lose you, or lose my boys," Becks cried. Connor placed his arms around his wife.

"I've got you, I won't let anything happen to you, to any of you. If the worst happens I'll take full blame. I'll tell them you had nothing to do with it, I promise you," he said, as he held her tight, her head resting on his chest.

Months had passed since they had last held each other, but now they stood in an embrace, feeling connected, finally feeling like a married couple again. Becks gazed into his eyes and they shared a passionate kiss, their lips meeting for the first time in what felt like an eternity. At that moment, she realised how much she longed to be close to him again. Becks intertwined his fingers with hers as they strolled inside together, shutting the door to the backyard. Leading him upstairs, she never once broke eye contact. Arriving at their bedroom she closed the door and kissed him passionately, exuding the innocence of a young girl's first kiss. He wrapped his arms around her, tenderly caressing her back with his fingertips. With gentle hands, he unfastened the buttons of her shirt, followed by her trousers. As she stood before him, adorned in pristine white underwear, she displayed an aura of pure beauty. His gaze shifted downwards, and he couldn't resist planting another tender kiss on her lips.

Taking his time, he removed his shirt, sliding it off one shoulder at a time, before proceeding to undo his trousers.

"Are you sure?" he asked softly.

"Yes, yes, I am," she answered, kissing him intensely. As he unclasped her bra and slid off her underwear, they shared tender kisses on their way to the bed. He laid on top of her, expressing his love, bringing her pure pleasure with each motion. He showered her with kisses, as she drifted into ecstasy, savouring the feeling of his touch. Entwined together, they lay on their backs, catching their breath after their intimate moment.

"I love you; I love you so much," Connor said, as he turned onto his side and looked at the love of his life.

"I love you, too. I want to get us back on track. Let's do it, let's move away like you said. Let's sell here and go, maybe to the coast," she replied.

"Really? I want us back on track too, this has been torture. A clean break from here will do us all good," he whispered, as he gently embraced her face. Their eyes locked, a connection that had faded with time, while his gentle touch traced her bare skin. With a sense of tranquillity, she surrendered to a profound sleep, a respite she hadn't experienced in months.

Meanwhile, as love blossomed back over at the Jones' house, Tamur Khan, the innocent taxi driver, was being interrogated.

"Mr Khan, thank you for coming to talk to us, we have some queries regarding your movements on Saturday 25 May. Now, you say that you picked Mrs Reed up from Cash Car at around 6:30 pm, and you dropped her on Tree Hill Road, just past Petal Lane. The issue we have is, from the point of her getting out of your cab, she hasn't been seen since. Do you see why we have a problem?" Detective McCabe asked.

"I don't know what more I can tell you. She got out of the taxi and walked downhill towards the housing estate. I didn't see any house that she went into or anything, she just walked. I turned the taxi around and drove out of the road," he said, in his broken English accent.

"So, can you tell me why you logged off so rapidly Mr Khan? Why the sudden emergency to log off duty at 6:48 pm?" the detective asked.

"I was due to finish at 7 pm, but I was tired, I had worked from 10 am that morning. My usual day is 10 am to 7 pm, so I decided to finish," Mr Khan answered.

"You see, Mr Khan, CCTV has you driving into the estate, we then don't have any eyes on you for a minute or so, and then we clock you driving back out of the road at 6:47 pm and you log off a minute later. We think that Mrs Reed didn't get out of your taxi. We think you drove into the estate, making it look like she got out. You, being a taxi driver, probably know that there's no CCTV on that part of the road; you locked the doors and she was stuck in the back of your cab," the detective implied.

"No, no, that's not true, I dropped her off, I did what she asked. She asked me to drop her on that road and then she walked downhill. The phone call, when I was driving back to the address, she rang someone, told them, OK, it's done, meet me at the house, or something like that," Mr Khan said.

"OK, we'll re-look into her phone records. Please know that we have officers searching your house and your car as we speak, Mr Khan, do you understand? You have the opportunity to cooperate with us now, Mr Khan, just tell us where she is!" Detective McCabe exclaimed, his voice resonating with an undeniable power.

"You won't find anything. I'm telling you the whole truth, I promise. She got out and walked off. Please, I haven't done anything," Mr Khan begged, desperately.

The following day, Mr Khan was still being held in custody while authorities searched his bedsit and car. Spending a night in a cell had left Tamur feeling furious, exhausted, and increasingly eager to escape.

"Good morning, team. So, last night a hair bobble was found in the rear nearside door of Mr Khan's taxi, and the lab has confirmed it's a match to Kerry Reed's DNA. Unfortunately, this doesn't give us any more evidence as we know Kerry Reed was in the back of his taxi. There was nothing in his house and nothing else in the car. He mentioned a phone call, but we've checked Mrs Reed's phone records and there was no call made at this time. The GPS from her phone was also lost at 6:47 pm and hasn't been turned back on since, which could coincide with the fact that Mr Khan disabled her phone. However, without any substantial evidence we can't charge him, and we're running out of time to hold him in custody," McCabe said. His voice and facial expression clearly revealed his disappointment.

PC King's eyes were fixed on the camera footage, his focus unwavering as he searched for any possible lead on the screen.

"Sir, I've checked the CCTV from Gillford Trading estate. You can see faintly in the background her getting into his taxi. I've attempted to zoom in as they travel towards Tree Hill, but his windows are tinted and there are no thermal cameras to allow us to detect body heat," Officer King said.

"Good work so far, team, but we have no option but to release him. Any more on those flights?" McCabe asked.

"I'm sorry, sir, there's nothing more. I'm awaiting the data on the flights going out from the local airports. As soon as I have this, I'll start to analyse it," Officer King said.

"Yes, keep me posted. Once this data is back, we need to make any visits we deem necessary. I have no choice but to release Mr Khan," McCabe disappointingly said.

McCabe's usual resilience seemed to waiver as he pondered over the investigation, convinced that he'd overlooked a crucial detail. Kerry's actions perplexed him, leaving him with a nagging suspicion that he'd failed to catch an important clue. McCabe entered Mr Khan's cell and released Mr Khan, a hard-working individual who dedicatedly sent money to his family in Pakistan. Collecting his personal items, Mr Khan left the police station, overwhelmed with a sense of violation and sentimentality. McCabe returned to his office. Puzzled, he sat at his desk and absentmindedly scratched his head while he sifted through the documents.

"What am I missing?" McCabe whispered to himself.

Later that day, after analysing information from three airports, they discovered a total of twelve individuals with names linked to, Susie, Suzy, Sue, and Susan T. It seemed like a stretch, but they decided to investigate every passport that had been used to board a flight. After checking the first ten individuals, they had no matches.

"This isn't looking good sir. I have two more," Officer King stated. The face on the next passport photo looked very familiar.

"Sir, have a look at this. What do you think? Looks a bit like her, right? Her name is Susie Trent," Officer King said.

"Possibly, what was her destination?" he asked.

"Paris, but there was a return flight booked for five days later," Officer King stated.

"Let's go and check it out. It's a long shot, but this woman might be leading a double life," McCabe said.

After travelling a distance of eighteen miles, they arrived at their destination and knocked on the door. To their surprise, a slender lady with long blonde hair opened the door, greeting them with a warm smile.

"Susie Trent?" Officer King asked.

"Yes, that's me," the lady answered.

"We're enquiring about a missing person. Do you know this lady?" Officer King asked, holding up a picture of Kerry.

"No, never seen her, sorry. Why have you knocked on my door?" she asked.

"We're just investigating anyone that may have been in contact with her," Officer King answered.

"Never seen her before but, to be fair, she does look a bit like me, doesn't she?" Miss Trent answered, letting out a low-pitched laugh.

"Yes, there is a resemblance. Would it be OK if we took your fingerprints, Miss Trent?" Officer King asked.

"Why? I haven't done anything," she answered sternly.

"We're not saying that you have. We just want to input your information to say that we've spoken to you, would that be OK? It will only take a minute," Officer King added.

"Yeah, I guess so. I haven't done anything, I swear," she panicked. The officers stepped inside the house,

"Do you have children Miss Trent?" Detective McCabe asked, as he cast his eyes over her untidy front room. With a narrowing gaze, his eyes appeared squinted, and a smell of stale smoke entered his nostrils. He endeavoured to detect any suspicious behaviour.

"Yeah, three. Two boys and a girl. They drive me crackers half the time," she answered, as she voluntarily gave the officers access to her fingers.

"What age are they?" Detective McCabe asked.

"Three, six and eight," she replied.

"You recently travelled to Paris, Miss Trent?" Officer King asked.

"Yeah, how did you know? I got engaged. My fiancé surprised me," she answered, as she smiled and looked at her engagement ring.

"Congratulations. Lovely news. Did your children go with you?" Detective McCabe asked.

"No, they stayed at their dad's house. It was his week to have them," she answered.

"What's his name, please?" the detective asked.

"Paul, Paul Smith. Why do you need to know this?" she replied.

"Just gathering information, nothing to worry about," the officer said, as he continued to ink her fingers.

"Thank you, you've been most helpful Miss Trent, we're sorry to have troubled you," Detective McCabe said.

They made their way back to the vehicle and headed towards the station. Officer King diligently examined the evidence and entered her fingerprints into the system.

"Not a match to Kerry Reed, sir. Her name is Susie Trent, it's not her," Officer King stated.

"Where the fuck has this woman gone?" Detective McCabe exclaimed.

"Wherever she is, she certainly doesn't want to be found!" Officer King replied.

"That's what scares me. People who are alive always leave a trace," McCabe replied. With a shake of his head and a nibble at his bottom lip, he expressed his growing concern.

On Monday, Becks wasted no time and contacted the estate agent. Their house was listed for sale by the end of the week and, surprisingly, they received an offer within just three weeks. It didn't take long for them to pack up their belongings and prepare for their new life in a home located seventy miles north from their current one. They had embarked on numerous journeys to inspect a selection of fresh properties, and had carefully chosen a spot on the coast, which happened to be a convenient fifteen-minute drive from Becks' parents' house. Becks resigned from her job and concluded her position in time for the summer holidays. Connor had decided to bring on a partner at his firm. Despite this, he planned to remain a silent partner as he established his new practice in their new location.

As the sun shone brightly in mid-August, the movers wrapped up the packing and hit the road for the start of their long journey. Ready to tackle the challenges of moving day, Becks and Connor were feeling positive. Their journey commenced as the boys settled comfortably in the backseat of the car, all packed up and ready to go. They passed by Tree Hill Road, catching a glimpse of the houses nestled down the hill, aware that Kerry's lifeless body rested there. Connor, Becks, Logan, and Rory were all set to embark on their fresh start.

They made a quick stop at the petrol station to grab some snacks for the journey. While her three boys selected chocolate and crisps, Becks patiently waited in the car. Connor paid at the counter and, as he turned, he was startled to find Detective McCabe standing behind him.

"Hello, Mr Jones," McCabe said.

"Oh, goodness, sorry, I was in a world of my own. Hello, Detective, how are you?" Connor asked, as he adjusted his glasses on his nose.

"I'm well, thank you. Are these your boys?" McCabe asked.

"Yes, Logan and Rory. Boys, say hi to the detective," Connor said, as he embraced them, wrapping his arms around their shoulders. McCabe's face let off a smile as he glanced down at the adorable little boys, sporting their glasses and matching polo shirts.

"They look just like you," McCabe said.

"Thank you. Did you ever find her, Detective?" Connor asked.

"No, afraid not. It remains a mystery, Mr Jones," McCabe answered, as he stared deeply into Connor's eyes.

"Very strange, Detective. Well, best of luck with it," Connor replied.

Stepping onto the forecourt, he secured the boys in the back seat before glancing up and exchanging a wave with Detective McCabe through the petrol station window. A smile and a nod from the detective greeted him back. Taking his place behind the wheel, Connor smoothly exited the petrol station, ready to continue his journey.

"Was that—" Becks asked.

"Yes, not found anything," Connor said with a grin. Connor gently rested his hand on Becks' leg before driving away from the town.

With the arrival of autumn, it had been three months since Connor, Becks, and their boys settled into their new home, embracing the opportunity for a fresh beginning once again. Logan and Rory were enjoying their new school and had already made a few friends. With Becks' parents living nearby, they were able to spend quality time with their grandparents and uncles.

Working remotely, from home, Connor successfully acquired new clients and was on the verge of finalising a lease for a new office space to launch his new firm in the upcoming year. While still a silent partner at his former company, he remained focused on progressing in a positive direction. Giving this fresh beginning his all, despite the differences with Becks' family, he discovered a newfound love for nature and made an effort to be more open-minded. Realising that life was about more than just material possessions, he embraced a simpler, more fulfilling way of life.

Becks made the bold decision to step away from work and take a well-deserved break. She chose to take the first term off after the children returned to school in September, allowing herself some much-needed time to recharge and focus. She utilised this time for self-reflection, cultivating a more optimistic outlook on life, enabling herself to recover from the recent traumatic events. By re-establishing bonds with her family, she became an integral part of their close-knit circle. This period of introspection allowed her to appreciate her upbringing and personal growth.

Connor and Becks had managed to rekindle the flame in their marriage, bringing it back on the path of happiness and harmony and it seemed that Becks had finally moved past the hurt of Connor's betrayal. She'd found it in her heart to forgive him and was determined to leave all the negativity behind. However, behind her loving exterior, she concealed a constant sense of caution, unsure if she would ever be able to fully let go and trust him again. To keep their love alive, they made it a point to have a monthly date night. Dropping off their boys at Becks' mum's house, they would spend quality time together, talking and reconnecting, reigniting the spark in their marriage.

As Christmas approached, they eagerly anticipated celebrating the holiday with Becks' family, making it their first Christmas together since before getting married. Ted and Mary paid their traditional visit on Boxing Day, delighted to witness their son thriving. The feeling of positivity returned to life, almost like the past year had been a dreadful dream.

Becks maintained communication with her ex-coworkers, who asked her to join them for a post-holiday dinner to catch up on her new life. During the New Year bank holiday, Becks visited Milton for the first time since relocating. Spending time with friends and staying at the Empress Hotel, the mix of emotions she felt left her feeling irritable, yet empowered. She drove by the rental house, finding everything peaceful before heading back on the two-hour drive to her family.

January marked the beginning of a new school term. Becks made her come back to teaching and found great joy in being back in the classroom. Taking on the responsibility of teaching year one, she relished the chance to be a part of the educational adventure once more, and cherished every moment of it.

As for Connor, his new firm started operating on 4 January. He wasted no time in tackling challenges and seizing opportunities as his business flourished. He felt a renewed sense of vitality, as if the past had been erased, with his wife, kids, and job all falling back into place. Life was looking up for him once more.

Saturday morning, after a hectic first week back after the New Year celebrations, Becks took the boys to her mother's place for the day so Connor could focus on work at home. As the friendly postman delivered the mail, a handwritten envelope caught Connor's attention. Perplexed, he set aside the rest of the letters and cautiously opened the mysterious envelope. As he unfolded the crisp white paper, the striking black font caught his eye, causing his heart to plummet. A surge of heat rushed through his body, while the hairs on his arms stood upright. His face turned pale with sheer horror.

The letter read, 'I know what you did to her. I won't stop until you are punished!' Connor read the words out loud. With no name at the bottom, he flipped the envelope to examine the front, where the ink stamp bore the word 'Milton' over the second-class stamp.

Gripped with emotion, he covered his mouth with his left hand as he crumpled the letter in his right fist. Panic consumed him as he hastily returned to his office, flinging the letter onto his cluttered desk before urgently dialling Becks' number.

"Hello," Becks answered.

"I need you to come home. Leave the boys with your mum and come home," he stated.

"Connor, what's wrong?" she asked.

"Just come home, now!" he exclaimed. Becks wasted no time, as she hopped into her car, embarking on the fifteen-minute drive back to their house.

Anxious thoughts raced through her mind, for the memory of the last time he spoke to her in such a manner was tainted by the grim reality that he'd taken a life.

"Connor?" Becks shouted as she entered the front door.

"I'm sorry," Connor said. As he walked down the stairs, he handed her the letter. Pure panic was evident on his face, and he appeared distraught and lost, unsure of how to comfort himself.

"Who's sent this?" Becks asked calmly.

"I don't know. The ink stamp says Milton. What the hell is this?" he replied.

"Listen to me, it's been over six months. If the police had anything they would be here, knocking on our door. This could just be one of her friends clutching at straws. I say we get rid of it, and we pretend that you never received it," Becks said calmly. She felt the urge to console him.

As she made her way towards him, she embraced him tightly, the wrinkled paper still clutched in her hand.

"How do these people know where we are?" Connor asked in desperation.

"I don't know. All I know is that the estate agent hasn't called. As far as we know, there are no issues at the house. I can call on Monday for a random spot check on the property. It's probably that couple who came to the house looking for her. They have nothing, we'd be the first to know if anything had been found," Becks replied, as she gazed affectionately into his eyes while clasping his hands.

"Did you drive by the house last week when you went to Milton?" Connor asked.

"Yes. Everything looked fine," Becks replied.

"I can't relive this. I thought it was over," Connor said.

"It is over, it is. We've moved on and we must never go back," Becks expressed strongly, as she held him close to her and smiled calmly.

During her lunch break on Monday, Becks phoned Wise Move to inquire about the tenants. Tony reassured her that everything was going well, mentioning that the tenants had welcomed a new baby boy and were delighted with the house, putting both Connor and Becks' minds at ease.

By May, there was no further news or anonymous letters, allowing them to finally regain some normalcy. On the night before Kerry's first anniversary, Connor was sleeping next to Becks when he suddenly felt a chill run down his spine. For the first time in months, he saw Suzy's face in his dreams. He woke in a panic, sweating and breathing heavily, startling Becks awake.

"Connor? What happened?" Becks whispered.

"I can't do this, I can't live like this anymore, the guilt is eating me alive. She keeps coming to me, she's there in my head, tormenting me," he replied with a cry. Becks gently wrapped her arm around him, offering a comforting embrace as she gently massaged his back.

"You have to, for our sake, you have to, there's no going back now," Becks replied. They lay down in bed and Becks smiled as Connor rested his vulnerable head on her chest, his eyes wide open and his mind haunted by his thoughts. A sense of dread lingered; he couldn't shake the feeling that this was far from finished!

Little did Connor realise that his affectionate spouse harboured a desire to maintain control. While Becks enjoyed her evening in Milton, she was the one who cunningly sent the anonymous letter. Under the cover of darkness she'd sprinted through the empty street, clad in a sleek black hoody. She couldn't help but smile as she slipped the letter into the awaiting post box, her mission accomplished. She intended to instil fear and remorse within him. She longed for him to be vulnerable so that he would suffer from his torment. She refused to let him escape the consequences of his wrongdoing, and was determined to make him pay for his actions.

Becks now finds herself transformed into a person she can barely recognise. The man she once loved so dearly has shattered her trust in him, however, she remains loyal to him, just as any devoted wife should. Nevertheless, she refuses to remain a victim. Unyielding in her pursuit of justice, she will ensure that he pays for his deeds until the end of his days, exacting her own form of retribution. Whenever he becomes arrogant and believes he has escaped the consequences, she will bring him crashing back to earth, maintaining his vulnerability. With newfound strength, she will forge ahead, reclaiming her life and embracing her empowerment. Gazing intently at her reflection in the bathroom mirror, she speaks to herself in earnest, "I am the captain of my destiny, and I choose to cherish every moment of my existence."